A LIFE
DIVIDED

(WHO DO YOU SAY I AM)
BOOK 2

DD ANDER
www.ddander.com

ISBN: 978-0-9953193-7-0 (print book)
978-0-9953193-8-7 (ebook)

RECENT TITLES
BY DD ANDER

I AM THE ONE

CONFESSIONS OF A FAST FOOD FREAK

<u>PLUS A NEW SERIES:</u>

THE 7TH CROSS (Book 1)

A LIFE DIVIDED (Book 2)

A LINE ONCE BROKEN (Book 3 . . . Soon to be released)

TABLE OF CONTENTS

PROLOGUE

THE LAST YEAR HAD PASSED as if a blur. For everyone. Janice was still grieving Jason's murder, and how quickly it had been dismissed by the authorities. Yes, he was a serial killer. And yes, he deserved to be in jail. But he didn't deserve to die the way he did. Perhaps her daily visits to the graveyard were unusual. So what?

Claire, Janice's long lost sister was now back in her life, and as an Investigative Reporter, had been instrumental in bringing her now deceased husband, Jason to justice.

Derek, the homicide detective and now fiancé of Claire, served as the lead investigator who ultimately tracked down Jason.

Janice's daughter Joline, had provided the missing link that would seal Jason's fate.

And Mikey, Claire's brother, would finally be freed after serving 30 years for murdering his father. He had accepted Christ as a young man while in jail, and was now an ordained man of the cloth.

But this morning when Janice arrived at the graveyard everything was about to change . . .

GRAVEYARD CONFRONTATION

J ANICE HAD GRABBED HER usual coffee and headed for the morning chat with Jason the same as she'd been doing for the past several months. Except this time there was someone else visiting at a gravesite a couple of rows down from Jason's. "Nothing unusual about that I guess." mused Janice, somewhat annoyed as she'd always been alone at this time of day.

The way the gravesites were arranged allowed her to stay in her vehicle while visiting, which worked well given the chilliness of the morning. She'd come to enjoy this morning ritual immensely. Hopefully the intruder would depart soon and leave them in peace. She felt guilty as soon as she thought it. "My God, who do I think I am?"

And then he approached her vehicle. Cautiously, she cracked the window open when he indicated that he wanted to speak to her.

"Can I help you?"

"I have a message for you."

"Me? What message?"

"Listen carefully. I'll only say this once. Return the notebook to us or your family dies. You have one week!"

With that he turned around and began walking away. "Wait! What are you talking about? I don't understand." And that was the truth. She didn't understand. How could she?

He strode back to her open window. "You know exactly what I mean!" He began to walk away again.

"Get back here! What are you talking about? I don't understand."

1

That's when he handed her a burner phone. "You'll be hearing from us. One word to anyone and your family dies! Got it?" She did.

He got in his vehicle and drove away. Janice collapsed back into her seat, shaking like a leaf. What the hell just happened? He'd just threatened her family. "Jason, what did you do? Oh my God!"

When her phone rang, she let it ring. She couldn't have answered it even if she'd wanted to. It was her sister, Claire, and there was no way on God's green earth that she could have kept her cool talking to her.

"That's unusual." Claire often spoke to herself. She was really beginning to wonder where Janice went each morning. "Maybe it's time for a chat after all. She's been acting a bit strange lately. Maybe she needed a shoulder to cry on or something. She always acts so tough but, God, you have to vent somewhere! Poor girl, I wonder what she really thinks?" Claire was in overdrive now. " Oh well, I'll try later."

Interestingly enough, the person Janice most wanted to talk to was Claire. And now she dare not. "Your family will die." and she began to cry hysterically. "I don't understand!"

The burner phone kept staring at her from the passenger seat where she'd thrown it. She flipped it over on its back yet it stared at her still. She covered it with a magazine. "There. What if he calls? Why is he doing this? Relax Janice, relax. Breathe." and finally she settled down as best she could. "What now?"

Wait. That's all she could do. Wait for a call and pray this was all a mix up. This was crazy; yet she knew it was real!

Claire tried calling yet again and still no answer. "OK, what's up? Alright, sister, I'm coming for you!" and with that, she jumped in her jeep and headed for Janice's home. "Nope, not here! Ok. Maybe Mom and Dad's." Janice's car wasn't in their driveway either, so rather than stop and make small talk right now, she headed for her next destination. She was pretty sure that Joline would be long gone by now but what the heck. It would only take a few minutes. But, once again, no Janice.

"Oh well, back to work. We'll catch up later." To herself.

Ironically, Jolene was also on the hunt for her Mom that very morning. She hadn't seen a lot of her this past couple of weeks and well, she was missing her Mom! Ever since the Jason fiasco, her Mom wasn't the same. Not that she blamed her, but I still need my Mom!

But, like Claire, she failed to find her Mom. Oh well, we'll catch up later. Maybe Claire's got time for coffee? A quick call which Claire didn't answer settled that issue so Joline decided it was time for a run. Then she'd stop in and see Grammy and Gramps. That was always a good time!

Janice's parents had always been steady as a rock. It didn't seem to matter what the issues were, they handled them all the same. Calm, cool, collected. Always with prayer. But this whole nightmare with Jason had really taken its toll. God how they'd prayed! Especially for their little girl! And for Jason's victims! What a terrible, terrible nightmare for all of them. How does one not weep? But they prayed for Jason too. May God's grace be sufficient.

Any work Janice had planned on getting done today was not going to happen. Not as long as that phone sat idly by threatening to destroy her world. "At least ring! Anything but this!" And it did. She gingerly picked up the phone and whispered into it. "Hello." Nothing. "Hello, is anyone there?"

"Listen carefully. I'm only going to say this once. I'll give you the benefit of the doubt that you don't know what I'm talking about, so listen up. Your husband took something from us and we want it back."

"I don't understand. When? Where? What did he take?" Janice was totally confused.

"I told you to listen. Now shut up!"

"I'm sorry."

Jason stole a small black notebook from the lady he killed in the park near Pine Street. You know what I'm talking about! I need it back now! Don't even think about going to the cops! I know where all your family lives, and trust me, I will kill each and every one if I have to. Have you got that?"

"Please don't hurt my family. I didn't know. Jason never told me anything. I'll look through his stuff. Please don't hurt my family. They didn't do anything!"

"You've never heard of "an eye for an eye? Jason took her out. We took him out, and if we don't get our notebook back, well, you know the rest."

"You killed Jason?"

"He deserved it. They would have got him sooner or later. We did you a favour!"

"Oh my God! I can't believe what I'm hearing!"

"Keep this phone with you and don't tell anyone. Find the book. I'll call back tomorrow. And don't try anything!"

The phone went silent yet again. She pushed it away from her, hung her head over the steering wheel and screamed as loud as she could. Thank God, she had pulled over in a deserted area when the phone rang. "Oh my God, what am I going to do?" But she already knew.

She headed home and parked in the garage. Hopefully she would be left alone. Jason's home office was much the same as when this all went down. The police had gone through it thoroughly, and if there was anything suspicious, she was quite sure they would have found it. They never said anything, not that they would've told her anyway, but she had no choice but to look for the notebook.

She began frantically searching through everything. Nothing! She did it again, and yet again, just in case. Still nothing. Her mind reeled as she searched. "Jason what the hell did you do?" Maybe she needed to call the police. This was crazy. Wait, maybe she could call Derek or Claire. They'd know what to do. But what if they're watching my family? I could never live with myself if something happened to any of them. Lord, please help me!

JANICE EXPANDED

J ANICE HAD BEEN COMING to the graveyard for the past year. A quick trip through the take out at Starbucks and then a casual drive to the graveyard to spend time with Jason. She knew that her family would be aghast if they knew, but this was her life. He was her husband. And he loved her. He couldn't beat his demons, but God, how he'd tried! And she loved him for it.

Some would say she'd lost it, that she was mentally unstable, and they could be right. But she didn't care what they thought. Thank God she was financially stable, and despite everything, her family still loved her. She knew they were watching her closely, but she had long ago learned how to turn on the charm and convince them of anything she wanted.

Except Joline wasn't buying it. Nor was Claire. These two often met to chat, and the conversation always involved Janice. They didn't want to alienate her, but they knew she was either not playing with a full deck or there was something else going on that they weren't privy to.

It should have been obvious to Janice that Claire, the investigative reporter, and Joline, her inquisitive daughter, would not let this rest. But it wasn't. Janice was off in her own world most of the time. But of course she was; she was a writer after all. A damn good one and that's where good writers lived!

Janice had begun what she coined Project X. None of her family knew of it and they wouldn't. Even after it was published, if it ever got that far. She'd already picked out the pen name she intended to use and had set up encrypted files just in case someone started snooping around. Now that her sister was back in their lives, and an investigative reporter at that, she'd make sure there was no trail to follow. Not only that, but her daughter and Claire had become pretty close this past year so it was imperative that she not arouse suspicion. Between the two of them, they'd pick it up in an instant.

Ironically enough, this whole terrible situation had not only brought her daughter home, possibly to stay, but had reunited her with a sister that she thought she'd lost forever! But they've got to quit blaming Jason for everything! We wouldn't be this tight knit family we've become if it wasn't for him!

She had to chuckle at her own words. Even to her they sounded absurd. Maybe she really had lost it. Too bad! I know him better than any of you!

But what Janice didn't know was that she was under constant surveillance. Not only observed but recorded as well. And not by her family. She had been for some time. Ever since Jason's sudden departure. And she also didn't know that the last word Jason heard before he died was "payback."

She felt, much like the others, that he was just another victim of jailhouse justice. They didn't like him. They had nothing to lose. End of story. But what she didn't know was that it was all a set up and the only reason she and her family were still alive was to put some time between the "incidents" so not to attract unwanted attention.

THE PAST YEAR

THE PAST YEAR WAS SURREAL. Mikey stood just inside the gate that would grant him his freedom. He merely had to walk through it. Claire had backed up her promise in spades. She knew the right people, and within months, his case was brought before a review board, and now, a year later, he stood at the door granting him his freedom.

He had fought Claire on this. This place was his life. He was living his God given purpose behind these walls. He was changing or at least contributing towards change in so many of the inmates. Surely this was God's calling on his life. But still, how could he ignore the one thing everyone in this place desired?Freedom. Even though many were unable to handle it once it was given, they still craved it, and he had to admit, so did he. But, he was scared. In here he was safe. He had to laugh at the absurdity of it all. With a final sigh, he stepped through the doorway and into the light. "Please God, help me find my way."

There they stood. Claire and O'Malley, with smiles as big as their hearts! They hugged, they laughed, and they cried. But this time the tears were tears of joy!

These two had left nothing to chance. O'Malley had plenty of room at his place. Mikey could stay with his as long as he liked. Truth is, he was probably more excited about it than Mikey. That old house was pretty darn lonely since his wife had passed.

And Claire? Well, she needed Mikey. She'd already cleared it with Pastor Rick. She and Derek had already set a tentative date; confirmation would depend on Mikey's release date. Tomorrow they would confirm it. Mikey would perform the wedding. Her Dad and Mom would give her away. Janice would be her bridesmaid. O'Malley and her boss would be the best men. And Joline would serve a few roles; that of flower girl, as well as songstress for them as they entered the chapel, and "unofficial" photographer.

Mikey, while indeed honoured at Claire's request, was seriously stressed. He would do her bid. But it would take every once of jam he could muster.

And even though he'd only been out a few days, he'd been getting calls from former inmates wanting to meet. And that would violate his parole. He knew he'd be tested and he didn't know if he'd pass. That was the only life he knew, and being out here was scaring the hell out of him! Why didn't Claire and O'Malley just leave things alone? What happens if I blow this?

What Mikey didn't know was that Pastor Rick was already hard at work on his behalf. He had long wanted to get involved in prison ministry but time and money never aligned at the same time. But with Mikey's knowledge of the prison system and of the true needs of the inmates, this may be exactly the right time!

He hadn't even mentioned this to Mikey yet in case it went nowhere. But after getting some positive vibes from the council, Rick decided that he and Mikey needed to talk. The pay would be substandard, which was no big surprise, but the possibilities to make a difference were endless. And that's something Claire had stressed over and over to him. Mikey was fighting getting out of the prison because he believed God was using him exactly where he was.

So Rick made the call. They agreed to meet at the Church. Mikey assumed Rick wanted to go over the details of the big day fast approaching. They made small talk and discussed the upcoming nuptials as expected. But then Rick dropped the bombshell. Mikey was stunned! "Are you saying that I can still work at the prison with the inmates, except that now I'll get paid for it?"

"That's exactly what I'm saying. It's not quite done yet but I had to share this with you. Both of us praying can't hurt! Of course, you won't be living at the prison but I'm confident we can work out something that'll give you as much access as you need. You get to continue your work but there'll be a lot more resources available to you. You in?"

"Am I in? Oh my God! Yes! Thank you God!" Mikey had to tell Claire. He was like a kid! And that felt so good. He had to tell her in person. "Claire, we need to meet. Right now." Claire was instantly alarmed. "Oh my God! What happened?" Funny how we always assume the worst. "No, no, it's all good. Can we meet?" "Ok, I'll be wrapped up in an hour and I'll drop by your place." "Don't be late!" He yelled into the phone before unceremoniously hanging up.

When Claire finally arrived Mikey was practically bouncing off walls! "What's come over you?" "Guess. Come on, just try and guess." Yep, he was definitely a kid again. Wholly crap! " Mikey, spit it out!" And finally, he told her and she pulled a Mikey! Now there were two of them acting like a couple of teenagers. That's when O'Malley walked in. "What the heck have you two been smoking?" They started laughing and before long, he had joined in. He had no idea what he was laughing about, but it sure felt good!

So they told him. "Thank you God! Mikey, I have to tell you, I was starting to get worried. I knew you were getting some calls, and as much as I hate to say it, the only people you know are either in jail or were in jail, and with your parole on the line, I was having my doubts whether this was going to work out or not. This is fantastic news!"

It was! But it would take time. Mikey was finding life on the outside a whole lot harder than on the inside. And O'Malley wasn't around all the time. But they were, and they weren't letting up!

Janice and Claire had become inseparable. Years that had been lost were recaptured as best they could be. But they weren't going to stay there. They were here and the time was now. They both marvelled at their parents. Janice remembered how heartbroken her parents had been when Claire walked out of their lives. Yet they had never spoken an ill word of her. And then how they'd welcomed her back into their lives without a second thought. But that really shouldn't have surprised them. These two were the very foundation that this family was built upon. They walked their faith day in and day out, and although hell may one day freeze over, this house would stand forever!

Claire would regale Derek with her and Janice's tales of shopping, and lunches, and memories of a time long since past. She giggled as she told him story after story, he patiently taking it all in. He loved seeing her this way! He chuckled as he remembered their first meeting. She was all business back then. All that mattered was "the story." Emotional? Not her! But now? He loved it!

The events of the past year had a profound effect on Joline. She was certain that she had her life planned out pretty well. Freelance blogger, travelling the world, getting involved in social causes wherever she felt she could make a difference, and generally just having a great time.

She still was, but the lustre had come off the apple. And like it or not, she missed her family big time! Maybe she'd better rethink this whole thing. Claire reappearing in their lives had really impacted her. Plus watching her Mom and Claire behaving like school girls, made her envious of not having a sibling! And maybe she should look into investigative reporting a little more seriously, after all, it wasn't like she didn't have connections!

BACK TO THE PRESENT

THAT'S WHEN THE PHONE rang and jolted Janice back into reality. It wasn't the burner phone. Thank God. But, it was Claire. Oh man, what'll I tell her? She'll know the minute she hears my voice that something's wrong. Ignore it. Stop ringing! And finally it did.

Claire was beside herself at this point. "Once, ok, I get it. You're busy. Twice, ok, maybe. But this is my third call and nothing? Something's wrong. I know it!"

And the bloodhound went to work. "Derek, I'm going to be late tonight, ok? I need to have coffee with Janice. I'll be home later. Love you." Message sent.

Message received. "No problem, I'll see if Roger has time to meet. It's been awhile. See you later, babe." Derek loved that Claire and Janice had become so close. Their story was almost impossible to believe and he got to see it unfold. Incredible!

Derek and Claire's wedding was fast approaching yet neither of them would cut down on their workload. They often spoke of this, but instead of treating it as a negative, they embraced it. They both loved their work! And, they got to work together after a fashion, but still retain their own identities and individual pursuits. It was perfect; for both of them.

Nonetheless, it was driving the wedding organizer nuts. But, if she thought she had issues, they were nothing compared to Mikey's. Poor Mikey! Claire's brother, recently released from prison after serving a thirty year stint for murder, was asked to perform the ceremony.

He had become an ordained pastor while in prison, where he felt completely at home, but now he was going to be front and centre marrying his long lost sister and her fiancé in a church in Seattle. How could he say no? My God, she had rescued him from a life sentence and all she had asked in return was for her big brother to officiate her wedding.

He reflected back to that time so long ago when he felt he had no choice but to kill their father. Either that, or Claire would have been their father's next victim. He had done what he had to do, but he knew the consequences. He paid dearly but Claire was spared, and unknown at the time, prison was the best thing that ever happened to him. My God, he'd met Charley, and what Charley had done for him was immeasurable. God had become real to him in that place. Thank you Charley!

But here they were. The wedding was only a few weeks away and even though he was honoured to perform the ceremony, he was even more afraid of disappointing Claire. She had done so much to win his freedom but he felt he was losing the battle against the onslaught of those who would hold him prisoner.

O'Malley was watching Mikey closely, and he was becoming increasingly afraid. Yes, Mikey was now a free man. He even had a pastoral position with the church which allowed him to continue prison ministry, which was great, but the outside world was proving to be every bit as ugly as anything that went on inside. And they had their eyes on Mikey. "We need you to be our inside man. You owe us. We're your brothers man! Didn't we protect you?" Short answer: No!

But the pressure was on and O'Malley knew it. And Mikey knew that O'Malley was watching every move he made. In one way, he appreciated his concern. In another, he resented that he was being treated like a delinquent teenager. And then he laughed. "Which I am, except that I'm 45 years old!" Thanks O'Malley.

Janice knew that Claire would soon ferret her out. Three unanswered calls from Claire would not go over well if she knew her sister. And she was getting to know her real well! "I'd better have something to tell her or this is going to blow up in my face. God, I wish I could just tell her everything. I need help. Maybe I'll tell her anyway." Janice muttered to herself as she worked.

"Yep, I'm telling her. She'll know what to do. Ok, I'm calling her right now!" And that's when the phone rang. Not hers. The other one. She sat staring at it and finally she picked it up. "Hello."

"Do you have it?"

"I can't find it. I've looked everywhere. I don't know where else to look."

"Keep looking! If I don't have it by tomorrow you'd better start saying your good byes!"

"Don't hang up! Please, give me some more time. I'm doing everything I can. Please."

"I'll call you tomorrow. If you don't have it, you'll find out how serious I am! And, don't you dare tell anyone or I'll kill them too. Got it!" And the phone went silent. Then the phone rang. She jumped but this time it was her cell phone. "It was Claire." What do I do now?

She'd better answer it or Claire would be all over her. "Hello?" with as hoarse of a voice as she could muster.

"Janice, is that you? Are you ok?"

"Sorry. I saw your calls but I've been down with a fever or something. I've been sleeping most of the day. I have a pounding headache so thought I'd just laze around the house. Never even went outside today. Sorry I didn't answer." To herself, God I hope she buys it!

Seriously? Like Claire would let it go that easily. "I'm coming over. I'll see you in ten." And then she hung up.

"Oh my God? I know. Mess up the bed. Hurry up." Talking to herself always worked. "Throw on my jammys. Mess up my hair. Wash my face with really hot water. Hurry!"

And that's what she did. "Oh, throw some magazines on the bed. Hurry up! What else? Oh yeah, turn most of the lights off. You're sick, remember." Dear Janice. Would it work? She'd know soon enough.

And then she heard the doorbell. "Drag yourself to the door." Janice was really getting into this. "I'd be fooled." She muttered to herself.

Claire burst in. "Oh, you poor thing. You look terrible. I promise I'll just stay a minute. I was getting worried. You know me. Always making a mountain out of a mole hill." And on she went. Janice had to laugh to herself. I did it! Or so she thought.

Claire had seen a lot of staged scenes in her day. Janice had done a really good job. No doubt about it. But now she knew something was up. And it was obvious that Janice wasn't about to let her in on it. Not yet, at least. Ok she'd play along. Perhaps next time she'd give her a few tips on how to really stage a scene. For now, Janice seemed fine. Let it go Claire. For the moment. But later, my dear Janice, the real work will begin. Don't forget who you're dealing with!

"Ok, baby. I'll let you rest. Sorry, I panicked, but you know me. Call me tomorrow, ok? Love you. Bye." Alright, what the hell is going on. Janice had been acting strange this last while but this? What the hell?

So of course she told Derek the moment she saw him. "Hon, there's something wrong with Janice. And I don't mean her usual weirdness. There's something else going on. I don't like it. My God, she even tried to stage her place to throw me off! That's crazy. I'm worried."

Derek, to the point as usual. "Ask her. But do it in person. You know that."

Of course she did but this was her sister. And she didn't want to lose her again! But she knew Derek was right. She'd do it tomorrow just as soon as she got her courage up. She almost had to laugh. She was known as a bulldog in the industry. Once Claire latched onto something she'd never let go. And now she was, at best, a Chihuahua. Way to go Claire!

Janice was frantic. "Jason, help me! This is all your fault! Come on." Uh huh. But he didn't, so she was on her own. "There has to be something. A key. A hidden compartment. Where is it?" (To herself of course). She almost had to laugh. A secret compartment in my own house. And I don't know about it? What next! But there was nothing funny about it. Hell, she'd feel better if she at least knew for sure that it was even here. Even if she couldn't find it! At least I'd know its true.

But all her ramblings and hours spent going through box after box produced nothing. And finally utter exhaustion forced her to call it a night. As expected, a very restless one indeed!

She awoke with a start, startled to see that it was "oh my God, 10:30! I need a shower." She had a shower, and then went back to work once again. "There's no use going through the same things over and over again. Think Janice, think. What would Jason do?" How was she supposed to know that? Hell, she didn't know he was a murderer either. Maybe he was a spy too, who the hell knows. And then she stopped. "Oh my God! What if he was?" And she began to panic.

She could hear it from the kitchen. The phone! And then it stopped. "No, no no! Please ring. Please, please. And it did. "I'm here. I'm sorry."

"Do you have my package?"

"Not yet but I'm . . ." and the phone went dead.

""No, please. Please ring. Please." But it didn't. And that's when she passed out. When she awoke she was on the floor, phone still clutched in her hand. She crawled to the sofa, hefted herself up, and laid down. "Just for a few minutes." To herself. And that's how she stayed for the next two hours.

But this time when she awoke they were in her house. "What's going on? Claire? What's wrong?"

"Janice, Derek's on his way over. We need to talk. I mean it!" Claire was steaming.

"I'm sorry." And the tears began to flow down Janice's face. Oh crap! Claire wanted to smack her but instead she cuddled her as one might a child!

THE ACCIDENT

SUDDENLY JANICE BOLTED UP. "Please tell me everyone's ok. Is everyone ok?" Claire's face gave her the answer she did not want to hear. "Tell me! Please!"

"Dad's had an accident. He's in the hospital but he's ok. Relax. Relax. Listen to me. Janice. Listen to me!" Claire was tough, no denying that.

"He's bruised up pretty badly but there's nothing broken. The Doctor said he's one lucky son of a gun. He should have been dead. Thank God he's in such good shape. But Mom's having a hard time. Harder than him I think. She's at the hospital with him."

"What happened?" Janice is back in the real world. "Tell me what happened."

"Apparently it was a hit and run. Dad was crossing the street by their place when this black car, he thinks it was black but not really sure, came roaring out a side street, never even stopped. Dad saw it at the last moment and tried his best to get out of the way, but it caught him around the hip area and flipped him through the air. The vehicle stopped, according to the eye witnesses but as soon as they approached, it took off. And, there was no license plate. That's pretty weird, don't you think?" She looked straight at Janice waiting for her reply.

And that's when Derek walked in. "Hi hon. Hey Janice."

"Hi. I need to go see Dad."

"I'll drive her." Claire piped up.

"I can drive myself."

"No. I'll take you. You're sick, remember?"

That sounded rather snide to Janice but what choice did she have? To herself. "It's all my fault. I'll never forgive myself! Thank God he's alive!"

"Ok. Let me get my coat." She didn't add "and my phones."

"You guys scoot. I'll lock up when I leave. I need to use the can." Which he did, but it wasn't the reason he stayed. This was perfect. As long as she was with Claire he could, dare I say it, snoop around a little. Janice started to protest but realized that it was a lost cause. She tossed her keys to Derek. "I have an extra set. I'll pick these up later from you."

And off they went. Janice praying for the phone to ring, and dreading that it would, at the same time. Claire watched all of this, and finally, exasperated, lit into Janice. "What the hell is going on? You knew something was going to happen, didn't you? Don't you dare hold out on me!"

Wow! Even with all the crap that had gone on before, Janice had never heard Claire talk like this. She was more afraid of Claire at that moment than the phone that began ringing as if on queue.

"Answer it!"

"I will. Please don't say anything. Please. I promised."

"Answer that bloody phone!"

"Hello?" Ever so meekly.

"I told you, didn't I? Next time, I won't miss!" And he hung up.

Thankfully they had arrived at the hospital. Claire glared at Janice. Janice stared straight ahead.

"Fine then! Let's go talk to Mom and Dad. And then we need to talk! Got it?" She got it alright. "Oh, and Joline will be back in town this evening. All she knows is that her Grandpa had an accident and that he's fine. That's all she needs to know for now. Agreed?" Janice nodded in agreement. "And" Claire added. "As far as Mom and Dad are concerned you don't know anymore than the rest of us. Right?"

"Right."

Dad was fine. Mom wasn't leaving his bedside, and anybody hearing the two of them would have swore that it was her in the hospital and him comforting her. Not the other way around!

DEREK DOES A LITTLE SNOOPING

DEREK WENT TO WORK. "Sorry Janice" under his breath, " but you gave us no choice." He had no clue what he was looking for but Janice's behaviour coupled with Claire's suspicion was good enough for him. He'd seen Claire's work up close and personal way too many times to doubt anything she said. And when her instincts kicked in, guaranteed, there was something there.

"It sure would be nice knowing what I'm looking for" he muttered as he worked. "Oh well, it's not like I haven't done this a time or two!" An hour passed before he decided he'd better get out of there before they came home, although he was pretty sure Claire would be interrogating Janice full core by now. Which she was.

If Janice had only listened to Jason she'd know exactly where to look. He'd tried to tell her but she had abruptly got up and walked out during the interview. All he wanted to do was protect her! He'd screwed up but he could fix it. He tried desperately to reach her time and time again from prison but she had refused to see him. And then he was murdered.

This whole thing was puzzling to Derek. Why now? He needed to talk; no, he needed to interrogate Janice. Sorry Claire. We're involved now. It's time to get serious! He knew Claire would try to intervene on Janice's behalf but their Dad could've been dead and it was starting to look like Janice was involved somehow, like it or not.

He'd speak to Claire first, but sorry dear, I need to do this my way!

Of course he should have known that Claire was thinking the exact same thing. The only difference was that she was already interrogating Janice right then and there in the car, over Starbucks lattes. If Derek was concerned about hurting Janice's "feelings," Claire felt no such remorse. This has got to end! Now!

Talk about feeling trapped! Janice was quite sure that even if she attempted to exit Claire's vehicle that suddenly the whole car would lock up and refuse to let her out anyway. "Crap, I need a lawyer just to keep her away from me!" She thought to herself. And then any resistance she felt disappeared and Janice told Claire everything. Even about the graveyard visits and the visit from the man in black. And about his threats. Everything. She trembled as she talked and Claire just wanted to grab her and hang on for dear life, but not now. Janice was talking and she wasn't about to interfere with that. Then finally Janice stopped, took a deep breath, took a sip of coffee, and began to sob silently. And that's when Claire wrapped her in her arms once again and held her as close as a Mom would hold a small child.

Quietly to Janice. "Now we can go to work."

Once Derek heard from Claire, he arranged to have a security detail on all parties involved, including Joline, even though she didn't have a clue what was going on. He'd explain it to her once she got home. She was much like Claire and it would take a small army to keep her contained. Too bad. Not your call! Sorry.

Claire dropped Janice off at her place with strict instructions to stay inside, talk to no one except family and don't go out under any circumstances. She and Derek would drop by later. "Don't worry. We'll get to the bottom of this. And take something for that flu." She began to giggle.

"Smart ass!" Janice burst out laughing as well.

"Hi hon. I just dropped off Janice. I told her we'd drop by later."

Derek bent down to give Claire a rather lengthy kiss. "Down boy, down." Oops. "Sorry."

"God, don't be sorry. I like it, but we've got work to do. I'm really worried about Janice."

"Me too."

Claire. "Ok, just so you know, I gave Janice the third degree this afternoon. I told her she wasn't fooling us one bit. And that's when she spilled her guts. It's bad." So she told Derek everything Janice had told her. " I'm pretty sure she told me everything, but the way she's been acting lately, who knows."

"Good. Now we can finally get to work. I searched her place high and low, and as far as I'm concerned there's nothing there. But if Jason had a secret hiding place, if you want to call it that, I doubt that he'd have it at their house. I know I wouldn't."

"You wouldn't? Is there something you're not telling me? Are you holding out on me?" she smirked.

But Derek was far too serious to play at the moment. "Seriously, if it were me, I'd have a safety deposit box somewhere, and I'd probably have it under an alias. I mean, that only makes sense to me. Don't you think?"

"Do you have an alias? Ok, sorry. Yeah, that makes sense. And we know that Jason was super intelligent. We all know that. And he had all those crosses. There's no way he would have had those laying around the house. I think you're right. I imagine that his old office was swept after he was arrested, right?"

"It was, but I'm thinking that I'd better have another look. If I'm not mistaken, I think it's still vacant. I'll check into it. I think you should start looking into the safety deposit box angle. Who knows? It might even be under his name. We have his bank info but maybe check with Janice. He might've had other accounts we don't know about."

"Joline should be arriving at the airport in about an hour. I think I should meet her. She'll probably want to head up to the hospital right away. She deserves to know what's going on."

"Fair enough. Just remember, you're family too, so they might be watching you as well."

"I will. Love you." Quick peck on the cheek and off she went.

Derek decided to head down to the office. If Jason was murdered by the same people that were now after Janice, this was taking a whole other turn. And they were looking for a black notebook. I need to look over that file once more. So that's what he did, and he'd have a whole lot more to share with Janice come morning.

Joline arrived. She freaked out as Claire expected. Then settled down. Asked a thousand questions. Big surprise. And then went to see her grandpa in her normally bubbly way. "Love that girl!" Claire to herself. She stuck around for the visit, keep it short you know, he needs his rest, which he did. And then, Joline blasted her all the way to her mom's house. "Yes. No. Uh huh. You're right. Should've told you on the phone. I know you're not a child. Blah, blah, blah.

When they pulled into the driveway, Joline was back to her composed self. She knew she needed to apologize for her outburst, but geez, I'm not a kid, for God's sake! But she'd take the high road. She didn't want to. But she did. "I'm sorry," and quickly exited the car. Claire waited until she was safely inside before heading to the sanctity of her own abode. At long last, she could have the bubble bath she'd been anticipating all day. She lit the candles, poured herself a glass of wine, and lay back in the oh, so hot water. Not a care in the world. Ok, not in her fantasy world anyway.

MIKEY TAKES A STAND

HAD SHE KNOWN WHAT was happening in Mikey's world at this exact same time she certainly wouldn't be in the tub relaxing. That was a guarantee. But she didn't know and she wasn't about to find out if Mikey had his way.

O'Malley was doing his best to protect Mikey but how does one babysit a 45 year old man? My God. He's out of prison. He's a good man. He's proven himself over and over. Back off! If he falls, he falls. It's not your fault. Of course he knew that, but he's a babe out here. And they're going to eat him alive.

Maybe. Maybe not.

Everyone knows there are gangs in prison. And everyone knows that business is still conducted from within the prison. It's a bit more difficult but everyone has their price and eventually pipelines are formed. One way or another business is going to happen.

If they could get to Mikey, and right now they were doubling down, they'd own the place. And he'd still be able to run whatever programs he wanted; they'd even participate. Everyone's happy, right? Not!

It was going to happen with or without him. But, if he didn't participate, they could make this place a living hell for anyone who dared have anything to do with him. People die in this place, you know. Your choice. You and Jerry were buddies, right? That kind of talk. Mikey was scared. Scared for Jerry and all the other inmates that he had grown close to. But if he gave in? Then he'd be no better than them. God, help me please! Anything!

But there are times when God seems exceedingly quiet and this was one of them. Charley, I wish you were here. I need you. As Mikey mulled all this over he already knew what Charley would do. Never give in to these guys, ever. Do it once and they'll own you. You already know that. They'll come at you hard but I have faith in you. You're stronger than you think. Come on man, you got me and God in your corner. What more could you want? Mikey shook his head at that one. It's true. What do they say? "If you got God in your corner you already have a majority."

Claire was up and at it at the crack of dawn. Hell, she'd even fallen asleep in the bathtub until the chilled water woke her from her slumber. Maybe that glass of wine did it. Or was that two glasses? Either way, she was feeling fine. "Here I come world. Get ready." Talking to oneself is great therapy. "I'm sure I read that somewhere." And that's when the phone rang. "Morning babe." Aww, her man checking up on her. "Love that guy." again, to herself. "Good morning my love!"

Hearing her like that automatically lifted Derek's spirits, and both knew this was going to be a very interesting day. And boy, were they right. "Lets meet at Starbucks for a quick coffee and set up our day, ok?"

"You bet, see you in ten." Claire was practically singing it.

And him. " I can't wait until we're married!"

Janice was still down for the count. Joline was pulling out her hair. This is so stupid! "Like I need protection. Give me a break! Claire, you'd better call soon or . . . or what, Joline? Agh!

So after coffee Claire headed over to Janice's place. Joline would probably be pacing like a caged animal. She couldn't help but giggle at the image. And Janice, much as she hated to say it, was probably still comatose. "Sorry sister." under her breath. "But sister, you got some big problems." And that's when Claire arrived, and sure enough, Joline met her at the door. She could tell that Joline was doing her very best to stay in control, so instead of saying anything, she gave her a long, heartfelt hug. That's all it took and soon they were in the kitchen sipping on the coffee Claire had so generously brought with her. "Is sleepyhead awake yet?" "I don't think so. I'm really worried about her. And now this crap. Is it ever going to end?"

"It is. I give you my word. Just hang in there with us, honey. We need you to be strong again. Your Mom needs you right now. I'm sorry your roles are reversed. She's lucky to have you." and with that Claire headed to the bedroom door. She didn't bother to knock. And there stood Janice, in the darkened room looking like a version of Frankenstein's bride. "This is ridiculous." She muttered to herself as she flung the curtains open. And then Janice began screaming at her. "Oh shut up! Grow up for Gods sake! We need to talk. Now!"

Joline heard it all. She wanted to jump in, but nope, Claire would probably attack her too. Forget that! She's a beast!

"Fine!" and with that, Janice followed her into the kitchen. Claire literally thrust the coffee at her, and that's all it took. A couple of sips and Janice had rejoined the real world. Now they could talk.

THE GAME PLAN

CLAIRE BEGAN. "We have a game plan. You need to know it. You're their contact so we need you to be in the game. Joline, I'm sorry, but you'll have to stay with your Mom for a bit until we catch these guys. Can I count on you?"

"Of course."

So she laid out exactly what Janice was to say when they called. The name of the game is stall, stall, stall. We need time. You have to buy us as much of it as you can.

They both nodded in agreement. Yep, Joline was all in. Time to go. And with that, Claire headed to the station to meet Derek. Before this morning was past they'd have a lead. Wait and see!

And they did. They'd went through the banking info they had on Jason. He did indeed have a safety deposit box. This could be the clue they were looking for. They made the necessary arrangements, broke open the box, and found . . . nothing. "Damn."

"I know we're looking for a notebook but let's not forget that Jason also had at least six crosses that we know of. Those had to be stored somewhere. I'm betting that it is a deposit box but I'm thinking it could be one he's had since he was a teenager. Think about it." Derek was on a roll now.

That's when Claire chimed in. "You're right. Jason murdered his parents in '94, right? Oh my God. Maybe his parents had a safety deposit box. Do we know anything about them? Where they banked, maybe?"

"That won't be hard to find out. He got the office on it immediately and within an hour they had all the info they'd need. Here it is, and the bank is still in business. Let's go."

This was almost becoming fun. Claire was in her glory, almost too much, in Derek's estimation. Oh well, at least they couldn't be accused of slacking it. As if that'd ever be a problem with these two.

"Yes, they did bank with us in '94. They did indeed have a safety deposit box but I'd doubt it still exists. Let me go check." which she did. "Sorry, it looks like it was closed shortly after their untimely deaths. Anything else I can do?" And with that Derek slumped back in his chair. "Crap." under his breath. "How about under the sons name? Or the mothers maiden name? Or . . . " Derek was not going down without a fight. Claire was liking his style more with each passing day.

So the clerk checked out the various combinations that they had come up with. And finally, when they were about to concede, the clerk had an idea. "Give me a moment. I have an idea." and off she went. And when she returned they could tell by her face that she'd found something. "I think this might be what you're looking for." And was it ever! "I've been her for thirty years you know. There's not many clients that I didn't get to know, especially back in those days. As I was going through those old files, it kept bugging me. I remember talking to Jason's Mom; he was only about three at the time, as I recall, and she had a most unusual request. Or at least I thought it was at the time. She wanted her own safety deposit box but it had to be in her and her son's names only. In fact, she used her middle initial and maiden name as main signature, with signing authority granted to Jason, which he could use at his discretion, anytime he chose. It's becoming clearer now. Yes, and her husband was not to know. I remember that. In fact, she arranged to pay for a full five years at a time. But, we were to never contact her. She came in from time to time. Well you'll see on the signature card. Here it is."

And there it was. Oh yes, the mom's signature from way back, but much more importantly, Jason's signature, time and time again! Last entry Dec 15, 2014. "We got him!" Derek was beside himself. "Oh my God! Thank you so much. I love you!" and he gave her the biggest hug ever. She'd been feeling pretty darn good playing investigator, but add the hug, and she was in seventh heaven. "And he was so handsome." she would gush to anyone who would listen.

But now it was time to open the box. One could have cut the tension in the room with a knife. They all gathered around. The clerk took the file key and inserted it in the lock, and with a flick of her wrist the key did its job. Now all there was left to do was open the lid. Derek and Claire looked at each other, and then he very slowly lifted the lid to reveal . . . a notebook. Nothing else. Oh my God! They gasped as in unison and Derek gingerly reached in and opened said book. And at that moment, they knew exactly what they were dealing with. And unknown to the man in black, the tables had now turned, and the hunter would soon become the hunted.

Then, as if prompted, Claire's phone rang, jolting them back to the present time zone and Janice, freaked out on the other end of the line, was screaming into the phone. "He's going to kill all of us! Please hurry!" and she hung up.

Claire and Derek just shook their heads. So Claire called Joline back instead. "Mom's freaking out."

THE NOTEBOOK

KNOW. TELL HER WE have the notebook. He'll call back. She needs to tell him that she thinks she knows where it is. She needs to convince him to wait until tomorrow. That's all the time we need. Don't tell her the last part. She might give it away. We need to copy the book before we part with it. Tell her to relax. We'll be by in a couple of hours. Thanks baby." and with that, Claire hung up.

The notebook was a literal goldmine. This was, without a doubt, an investigative reporters dream come true. Claire was over the moon. Derek had seen her in action before, but this? Wow! She was practically frothing at the mouth.

She tried to contain her excitement but this was her DNA, she lived and would die for this stuff. For a moment she sensed Derek's disapproval. Oh my God. He's disappointed in me! Doesn't he understand what a coup this is?

The truth was that Derek was shocked by her behaviour; maybe disturbed by it, would be more accurate. But he soon shook that foreboding off and got on with the business at hand. He realized, as did Claire, the ramifications of their find. But that's where they parted. He couldn't run amok with this stuff like a reporter could. This was the kind of arrangement that made them a great team but it was also a dividing point between them. And right now, it was paramount that they get this notebook copied in its entirety, and then turn it over to Janice to get the blackmailer off her case.

The only real case Derek had to work with at this juncture was the threat, or perceived threat against Janice and her family. What proof did he even have that it was real? Of course, he didn't mention that to Claire. After all she was with Janice for one of the calls. But the way Janice has been acting lately? Let's face it. She could have made the whole thing up. Ok, not the hit and run, but that might be an entirely separate event. "Oh boy." to himself.

Claire, on the other hand, was chomping at the bit. The moment she had a copy in her hands the real work would begin. This would be the story of the year, no doubt about it! She wanted to call her boss then and there but refrained from doing so. Derek looked peed off enough already. And if it was at her, then they had some talking to do!

All Janice could do was wait for the next call. She had the notebook and she wanted it gone as quickly as possible. And now, instead of dreading his call, she waited anxiously for it to come. "Please ring. Please."

She knew that they thought she was going crazy. But, she wasn't. Let them think whatever they want. Hopefully, this madness would be over soon and they'd all go away. Even Joline. "I need my space. Besides, my project is important too, you know!" To herself.

Joline was thinking much the same. "Once Mom is okay, hopefully soon, I'm out of here. I have a life too, you know." She found it hard to believe that she'd been thinking of settling down in Seattle. "I think I was just caught up in the moment. I'll just make a point of coming home every few months. That makes more sense. Besides, Granny and Gramps want me to live my life. They must've told me that a thousand times!"

No one had bothered to tell the grandparents about the supposed attempt on their lives. That would be on a strictly need to know basis, and they didn't need to know. In fact, Derek was wondering if there was anything to know anyway. Still, they took it seriously, and had assigned an undercover officer to the case, albeit discreetly. It wasn't like the old folks ventured very far anyway, and since he was being released from the hospital today, they'd be heading home and staying in for the next few days regardless. This whole thing will be over soon anyway. At least, it'd better be.

As it turned out they never did identify the vehicle involved and soon it was added to file thirteen. Gramps was back to his old self, but when he went for a stroll, he was a whole lot more cautious than before the accident.

Derek had arranged for the notebook to be copied. Now both he and Claire would have a copy. After a preliminary look he could see why Claire was chomping at the bit. Heads were going to roll, no question, but he didn't want it to be hers! These are dangerous people. People disappear when they cross these guys. He didn't like it. Not one bit! They were going to have to have a very long talk.

Claire called her boss to fill him in on the latest developments. He was on board immediately but with his customary warning which she'd heard a hundred times. "Your life is worth more than the story. Never forget that." She knew that but sometimes the stories were bigger than any one person. She didn't say that to him. But he already knew that.

But for now she needed to connect with Derek. They needed to get the notebook into Janice's hands and instruct her on how to handle the next phone call. This was going to get dangerous. The blackmailer needed the notebook but he also needed the witness "gone." It was imperative that Janice understand exactly what had to happen. "Either he makes the rules or you do. You have the book. He needs it. You're in control whether you know it or not." Derek emphasized each word as he spoke. "Do you understand?"

"Yes." Does he think I'm an idiot or something? I really don't like you!" To herself.

So they laid out their plan. There would be minimum danger as long as Janice stuck to the script. And for the fiftieth time. "Got it." "Yes, I've got it." Get out of my face! Claire said nothing but watched Janice intently. She could see that she was seething inside. It was best that she stay out of it. Derek knows what he's doing. And now they'd wait. For as long as it took. What choice?

The hours dragged out. The cell was silent. "Why hasn't he called? I thought he'd call again last night. This is creaking me out!" Janice to no one in particular. Joline was nearing rage status. Derek was clearly bored. Claire's mind was on the notebook, and Janice wanted to be with Jason. And then it rang. They all looked towards the phone and then Derek nodded to Janice. She picked it up. "Hello?"

"Do you have it?"

"Yes."

"Ok, here's what you do. You"

"No. I don't trust you. I have the notebook. You want it. You listen to me."

"How dare you? I'll kill all of you. I'll . . . "

"Fine! I'm calling the cops right now!"

"Wait! Calm down. Ok, fine. Give me the notebook and you'll never hear from me again. I promise."

Janice was doing a great job. Derek passed her a note with some instructions. She passed those on to the blackmailer and the drop was arranged.

"If you double cross me, I guarantee you'll all die, every one of you!"

"Just take your book and get the hell out of my life!"

And that's what happened.

The drop was made. The blackmailer had sent a series of runners. One to pick up the package. A kid on a skateboard. He quickly passed it on to another several blocks up from the drop, and he did the same. Four times in all. The cops thought they had this covered but weren't expecting a bunch of kids to be involved. Of course they corralled the kids but by that time it was too late. Hell, for fifty bucks a pop, all they had to do was deliver the package a couple of blocks to the next boarder. Easy money. Besides, they were all underage. Whatcha going to do to us anyway?

As far as Janice was concerned, it was over. "Now get out of my house. Not you sweetheart." To Joline. "As for you two. Why are you still here?"

They were every bit as glad to be gone as she was to get rid of them. Finally, a win win! Now she could get back to Jason! And the moment they were safely out of earshot, they glanced at each other and began to giggle. And then roar. And at the same time."Family!"

MIKEY AND O'MALLEY

MIKEY WAS PRAYED OUT, if there was such a thing. He'd prayed. He'd listened. But the silence was strangely deafening. "Come on God. Give me something. Please."

And of course God did. In the silence Mikey found the answers he needed. He knew what he had to do. It would take courage but he took solace in Charley's words so long ago. "You are so much more than you think you are. And never forget, you have God on your side." "Love you Charley. Sure wish you were here."

He knew this would not go over well. He also knew that Jerry would likely die unless . . . Maybe there was a way. "O'Malley, can you meet me? We gotta talk."

O'Malley hung up the phone."Yes! I knew he could do it!"

So they met down on the water front where O'Malley had taken him sailing. Once. And that was enough, thank you very much. Claire may have been a sailor, but he wasn't and he wasn't about to become one. Forget that nonsense.

Mikey filled him in on everything that had happened since his release. Everything. Every detail. He did that on purpose. That way he couldn't "pretend" it didn't happen. Now O'Malley knew as much as he did. Plus, O'Malley had connections that he'd never have. But, Mikey had established quite a reputation while on the inside. Between the two of them, and you know who, they just might be able to move a mountain. They were certainly going to try.

And at midnight that very night, a prisoner was escorted from his cell under armed guard, and delivered to a holding facility several hundred miles distance from his former home. "What's going on? What'd I do? You can't do this." Really? We just did. Said the guard.

The prison was abuzz the next morning. They were all accounted for, save one, and no one was talking. "Where's Jerry?" And then they knew. But soon all hell would break loose!

"Jerry, you have a visitor."

"Who?"

"You'll see. Come on."

"Mikey. What the hell?"

"Hey Jerry. Sorry about all the drama but I had to get you out of there."

"What are you talking about? You did this? Why?"

"Because you'd be dead if I didn't, that's why."

"Are you insane? Those are my friends!"

"No they're not. They were going to kill you, man, just for being my friend. If I didn't go along with their plans, you were toast. I had to do something."

Jerry sat for a long while trying to comprehend what Mikey was telling him. Finally. "They wanted you as their outside man. That way they'd control the entire prison, right? They almost do anyway. Why didn't you just go along with them. Man, you coulda been rich."

"Jerry, you know me. And you knew Charley. I couldn't do it, man. I would've been selling my soul. And I couldn't leave you there. You're my friend. I did what I had to do. It's going to get ugly there but at least you'll be safe."

Jerry hung his head and began to sob. "I've never had a friend like you. You did this just for me?" Tears streamed down his face.

"I had to. You're a good man, Jerry. And you're my friend."

And soon it was time to go. "We'll stay in touch. I promise." And they would.

JOLINE MAKES HER CASE

"**M**OM, CAN WE TALK? Not about this stuff. Are you up to it?" Joline needed to vent.

"I suppose you're going to tell me I'm crazy too. Is that what you want to talk about? I don't!"

No, Mom. I just want your advice. I miss our talks."

"I'm sorry baby. I shouldn't have said that. It was a lousy week. Thank God it's over! Of course, sweetheart. Anytime."

"Thanks Mom. I've been doing a lot of thinking lately, and I think I need to get on with my life. Follow my own dreams, you know. You know all my crazy dreams, right? I kind of stuffed them all back in the box after, well, you know why. But, I don't think my life is supposed to be here."

"I agree."

"You do?"

"Absolutely. I've been meaning to talk to you about that. Time passes way to quickly and suddenly you can't do the things you wanted to. You're married, or there's kids, or you get sick,or whatever. Baby, you have to live your life, whatever that means to you."

"Wow. I wasn't expecting that. Wow. That's all I needed to hear. Love you Mom." And that's when she wrapped Janice in the biggest bear hug ever. Tomorrow she'd begin planning her new life. Yes!

And so would Janice. Of course Joline needed to live her own life. And besides, it would be good for her to put some distance between her and Claire. "That's what I'm going to do!" She was still peed at the two of them. " Smart asses!"

It seemed everyone had been a little too close for comfort these past number of days, and distance would be a good thing, at least for a time. They say absence makes the heart grow fonder. They also say: time will tell. Guess we'll just have to wait and see.

THE MADAM

I T SEEMS OUR MADAM was up to more than just taking names and numbers of her preferred clientele. The details contained therein were not only of an intimate nature but detailed financial activity that should have never seen the light of day. In fact, if Derek was right, this notebook was bound for someone else's hands long before Jason came on the scene. It looks like he'd simply picked the wrong victim. Ironically, he may have served the greater good despite himself.

Claire was also going through said documents at her home. She and Derek could have been doing this together but he would've put a damper on it. Sourpuss! She wanted to enjoy every moment of it and he was, well, a grouch.

Neither one of them was willing to admit that this was more than a hiccup. They'd both been working extremely hard on this case. Family was involved. They were tired. They needed some space. From each other.

Derek sat alone in his office pouring over the documents, making notes as appropriate. He ordered in a pizza. And that's where he stayed for the evening.

Claire turned up the music, poured herself a glass of wine, ran the bath, lit the candles, and prepared to settle in to read the same book as Derek.

Tomorrow they'd compare notes. One would set about working with the data they could legally use. The other would begin to dig and probe into very dark places. Ultimately they would need each other. For now they would work together, but alone.

IT'S MIKEY'S FAULT

H E STARTED HEARING ABOUT various inmates "accidents" that were occurring at the jail. Not officially, of course. Grapevine stuff. Unreported stuff. It seemed inmates were running into doors at an alarming rate, or tripping and falling into tables and such. Nothing really serious but at least three of the inmates ended up in the dispensary with cracked or broken ribs. The rest, well, when you run into a door you're going to get a black eye . . . or two. Aren't you?

Mikey knew it would come to this, in fact, he had no doubt it would get a whole lot worse. Probably about the time of his first official visit. That was only a week away. Preparations were already underway. Security would be doubled for the occasion. The last thing the prison needed was someone snooping around. And we're not just talking about the inmates here.

Mikey had sought council from Pastor Rick, as well as various others who worked within the prison system in a similar capacity. The advice was always the same: either you'll blink first, or they will. It has to be them. There can only be one alpha. Don't ever forget that!

He knew that better than most. None of them had ever been in prison except as a visitor or in an official capacity. He'd been an inmate for nearly thirty years. Yeah, it was safe to say that he knew a bit about how it worked. In fact, that's what made this particularly dangerous. He knew too much. And not just about the inmates. It wouldn't surprise him one bit to find a door that suddenly unlocked for no reason, or to find himself alone in an unsupervised area. Not one bit!

Those on the inside who dared called Mikey a friend, stuck to-gether as best they could. This thing could explode at any moment and they knew who the targets would be, and there wasn't a damn thing they could do about it. Protection? In here? Right! Half of the guards were as crooked as the inmates.

And of course both sides reached out to Mikey. Different mes-sages of course. "Whatever happens is on you, Mikey! Don't ever for-get that!" But then from the other side. "Tell our story Mikey. Let the world know. It's our only chance!"

Betwixt and between is where Mikey lived. The butterfly had flapped its wings and now the tsunami was imminent. How much damage would occur was anyone's guess. But, one thing Mikey vowed, when the waters receded he'd still be standing. Count on it!

CLAIRE BEGINS TO PROBE

CLAIRE AND DEREK MET as agreed that morning. They were an interesting couple, these two. Obviously in love, but also obvious of each other's space, or boundaries, if you will. If they could maintain that they just might have a chance.

They compared notes. Of course, Derek would stick with the current investigation but only to the degree that they'd let him. After all, he was in the cold case division, remember? They were simply extending him a courtesy because of the family involvement. Claire, on the other hand, could fly with the eagles if she dared. And that's what bothered Derek the most. Knowing Claire, she'd fly far too close to the sun.

And as far as Claire was concerned, Derek had better get used to it. She had wings for a reason, and it wasn't just for show. Besides, the ground was already littered with turkeys, thank you very much. So she dug, and the more she dug the more filth she uncovered. There was far more than one story here. Dozens in fact. Poor Derek. He's going to have a fit! She involuntarily snickered. "I am so bad." to herself of course.

DEREK THE COLD CASE COP

EREK REVISITED THE STREET cameras in the area where the hit and run had taken place. He wasn't fully convinced that they were connected with the notebook but he'd long ago learned that "coincidence" was rarely "coincidence." And besides, he may have been letting his prejudices get in the way. Just a little. It wasn't that he didn't like Janice, but this past year had been pretty strange, and anything she did wouldn't have surprised him. Nonetheless, here he was.

And the cameras revealed . . . "Wait a minute. What's that?" He zoomed in closer. The far bottom of the back window bore a sticker of some sort but it was far too fuzzy to read. "Maybe the lab guys could clean it up a bit. At least it's something." He made the call. Probably nothing but he'd know later on this afternoon.

That's when Derek decided he'd better get back to doing his own job. There were a lot of cold cases that needed his attention. He might just be one cold case cop, but he had a job to do, and there were a hell of a lot of hurting people out there counting on him to find the perpetrator(s) who took their loved one(s) away from them. And it was best he not forget that.

But there was one item that seemed to be getting short changed with all the craziness going on these past few days. The wedding. Oh yeah, there was supposed to be a wedding. Remember? Both Claire and Derek had been getting numerous calls from the wedding planner, and both had kept putting her off. "Not now. Sorry. Later. Honest."

No one could blame her for wondering if they were even going to go through with it.

So Claire called her. "You're calling me? You've called off the wedding! Please tell me you haven't called off the wedding! Oh my God!"

"Take a breath, girl. Geez. Relax, ok. No, we haven't called off the wedding. We told you we'd get back to you. So here I am. What's up?"

Oh that helped. "What's up? Oh my God! What's up? Everything's up. That's what's up!"

All Claire could think was "Holy crap! We should show her a dead body or two. Wouldn't that be fun to watch." To herself. "Claire, be nice." And then she played nice the next two hours pacifying the planner. "My God. If that's what I had to do for a living, I think I'd shoot myself!"

And on impulse, she called Mikey. "Hey bro. How are you? We haven't talked in a while."

He chuckled. "Yeah, it's been a crazy time alright. Are you calling about the wedding.?"

"Not really. I mean, yeah I guess in a way. We are still getting married, you know. In case you were wondering."

"Nope. I wasn't wondering. How are you baby sis?"

"Baby sis. Wow. I'm fine. Yeah, we're fine. Just crazy busy all the time. We need to do coffee soon, k? Just the two of us."

"I'd love that! When?"

Oh great Claire! You and commitment. Uh huh. "How about right now?"

"Absolutely! The usual place. I need thirty minutes. Ok?"

"See you there." Take that. "Can't make a commitment, hey?" She loved these one sided conversations!

Janice made an entry in her day timer. It was simply stated: Today you take back your life! Yes! As much as she'd miss Joline, she needed to go. For both of their sakes. Mom and Dad were no big deal. At least they weren't always trying to tell her what to do. Claire, well, she's ok, but we need some time apart. She's way to damn snoopy!

And with that she headed for the door. "Come on in sunshine."

And there stood Derek, about to ring the doorbell. "Well thank you. I never knew you called me sunshine. I kind of like it."

She stood stunned. He burst into laughter. "I'm sorry. I just swung by to drop off your keys. Remember, I have your spare set."

"Oh yeah, sorry, I forgot. I was just on my way out."

"That's fine. I'm not staying anyway. I just didn't want to misplace them. Anyway, here you go. Have a great day." And with that, he was off.

"Hmmm. That went well. Ok." To herself. "Actually I do like him, but why does he always have to be so damn happy?" And then she chuckled to herself. "Guess it could be worse."

She felt nervous as she made her way to Jason's grave. She couldn't help but survey everyone around her just in case it was him again. It creeped her out. But she'd given him what he wanted, so she should be safe. "It's not like I really have to visit Jason." Under her breath. "To hell with it! I'm going." And she did. They had a great visit. Like always. " And if you don't like it, stick it in your ear!" To absolutely no one.

CLAIRE AND MIKEY'S COFFEE DATE

S O CLAIRE STARTED. That may have been a mistake. For the next half hour she barely came up for breath. "It's your own fault! You insisted I start first!" And they burst into laughter. God, it was good to laugh! And then she continued. With each new revelation Mikey became more and more concerned. These weren't choir boys we're talking about here. These people kill people. Claire, what the hell are you doing?" He didn't say it but he was certainly thinking it. And if she ever gave him a chance to speak, he'd tell her. Then, finally, she quit talking. He waited a moment, in case she was just catching her breath, but no, it was his turn. Thank you.

So he let her have it. One barrel after the other. All she could think was : another Derek! Why did I say anything? Men! These guys would be happier if I stayed home and baked them a cake! Geez! It's no wonder I don't tell Derek everything! She was not a happy girl!

As far as Mikey was concerned that was just too damn bad! She was a bully. Plain and simple. No wonder she got to where she was. "Derek, I think you're nuts!" Ok, he didn't really think that, but she was definitely pushy. I doubt there is one person alive who wouldn't agree with that! He was probably right.

"Claire, I wouldn't be saying these things if I didn't care. You know that. Derek must be freaked right out. He wants to marry you; not bury you, for Gods sake!"

Claire had calmed down by then as well. "I know. But please try and understand me, ok? You're following your passion, right? Or God's calling on your life, however you want to say it. That's what I'm doing too. I was born for this stuff. I love it and I'm damn good at it. And ,like your profession, it changes lives. Someone has to do it. Mikey, I have to do this." And with that, she went silent. Certainly not the Claire he knew. But, he also knew she was right. He'd support her. Of course he would. But try not to worry? Fat chance of that!

And then Claire piped up. "I heard a rumour, Mikey. About you. Fill me in, ok."

Mikey glanced at his watch. You know what sis, I'd like to, but I have an appointment shortly. It'll take too much time. Let's meet again real soon, and I promise, I'll tell you everything. No sense trying to hide something from you anyway. Right?"

"Right. Ok, big brother. Love you. Be careful out there."

"Maybe you should follow your own advice, you think? Love you sis."

MIKEY'S PRELIM VISIT

THEY WEREN'T EXPECTING HIM. And that's what he wanted. If there was to be an element of surprise, he wanted it on his side. So he arranged a meeting. He and Big Ed. One on one. No warning whatsoever. It wasn't like a prisoner could refuse to see him. Besides, it wouldn't look good to the other inmates if he refused to meet Mikey. Put up or shut up time.

So they met. After the usual threats they settled down for a chat. Mikey laid it out as best he could. One way or another it was going to happen. If he was smart, he'd be on board when this went down. If not, well, a transfer could be arranged. For one person. Guess who?

"You can't do that. I have my rights. My lawyer'll bury you, if I don't first!" These guys were always so tough. How Mikey wished they'd just let him go a couple of rounds with some of these jerks. He had to laugh at the thought of it. "Just a friendly boxing match. You know, to entertain the boys." Uh huh, likely story.

"You must have known that I couldn't be bought. How couldn't you know?" Mikey wanted an answer. But then he had his ah haw moment. "You're not in charge anymore, are you? That's it! You're yesterday's man. This interviews over!" And with that Mikey got up, slammed the book shut and headed for the door.

"Stop! Wait. Let's talk. Can you get rid of the guard?" He whispered just enough for Mikey to hear. "And the camera and recorder?" Interesting.

It only took a moment. "We only have a couple of minutes. Say what you have to say."

"Ok, you're right. George's in charge. He'll kill me if he knows what we're talking about. You gotta protect me. You can do that, right?"

"Why wouldn't George meet me if he's the big dog in here now?"

"He's got something up his sleeve. I think I'm being set up as the fall guy. We were supposed to kill a couple of the guys when you showed up next week. And do our best to cause a riot. We knew some of us would be taken down. Not me supposedly, but I think I'm being set up to take the hit. Then once everything settled down, he'd step up. If you think I'm bad, I ain't nothing compared to him and his boys. I'm as good as dead if anybody finds out I told you this. You gotta promise me, man. I can help you."

Mikey had rolled the dice, and unbelievably, won. This could work. He'd managed to get Jerry out of there. This dude was a huge fish in this pond. Claire liked her coups. Well, so did he!

"Ok. We can work out something. Tell George that everything is set for next week. Tell him I was just ensuring your co-operation when the big wigs arrive next week. And be ready to go. Don't say a word to anyone. He's gonna be suspicious. You're gonna have to keep your-self alive until then."

"How'll I know when you're coming for me?"

"You won't. That way they can't even beat it out of you, right?" Sounds sick but that's just the way it is.

They both knew that what he had said was true. Jailhouse justice and all.

Mikey could hardly believe what he was hearing. And he could hardly wait to get out of there. Oh my God! This was incredible. Of course, he'd have to remain grim faced until he got outside these walls. Which he did, but once he got back in the car and was safely out of sight of any prying eyes, he screamed at the top of his lungs. "Thank You God!" And then the tears began to flow and he had to pull over. He'd gotten his answer. In spades.

THE GRAVEYARD VISIT

J ANICE AND JASON HAD a wonderful visit. She drank coffee and told him everything that had happened these past few days. She talked. He listened. She liked this arrangement. He didn't care. Whatever makes you happy, Janice.

And that's the way it would go, day after day. Derek had checked on her a couple of times, but always from a distance. He didn't mention it to Claire. He knew what she'd do, and well, he was staying out of it. She could check for herself if she was that curious.

But what no one knew was that Janice was busy at work on her new book. She'd never written to adults before, and she'd never even contemplated writing about, of all things, murder. But then she hadn't planned on marrying a serial killer either. And if there wasn't a story buried in there someplace, then she was definitely not a writer. But of course she was. Just like he was a serial killer. But he was much more than that. They'd see soon enough.

One thing about Janice that set her apart from a lot of other writers was her ability to inject herself fully into the story. Even her children's books contained her DNA, and of course, Joline's.

Her family thought she was losing it, and for a time so did she, but it was necessary to plumb the depths, so to speak, to understand the character she was trying so hard to bring back to life. She had to admit that at times she even scared herself. No matter. It would be worth it in the end.

It became apparent that Janice needed to interview a psychiatrist or two to validate the conclusions she appeared to be reaching. She was obviously quite adept at handling the role of the psych patient. No further work would be required in that area.

AND THEN HE WAS GONE

GEORGE NEVER KNEW WHAT hit him. He'd set the whole thing up. Even had it arranged so Big Ed would take the fall. So what if a few of the inmates died along the way. He'd just wait for the dust to settle and then take over. Everyone knew he was in charge anyway; Ed was yesterday's man and everyone knew it.

So when he was suddenly summoned to attend the meeting with the pastor and the V.I.P.'s, he knew something had changed. "Ok, play dumb. They don't know nuthin'."

But it turned out they did know something. In fact, they knew a whole lot. About him and about the pipelines in the prison and beyond. And Big Ed was nowhere in sight. "Where the hell was he? Crap!" To himself. "Don't say a word. Deny everything. I'll kill him! Where is he?"

"By the way, you're being charged with running a criminal organization, along with four of your so called gang. And since you're the Big Dog around here, you might as well hear this from us: three guards have been relieved of their duties. I'm sure you know their names. They certainly know yours." Barry, the lead detective on the investigation, was enjoying every moment of this. He'd been investigating the prison pipeline for months but was getting absolutely nowhere. And then the pastor called. And suddenly it was a new ball game.

Moving Big Ed out of the prison at the exact same time as they arrived was brilliant. Strategically moving the meeting ahead by four hours ensured there'd be no leaks. It went off brilliantly. And the pastor coercing Big Ed to cough up everything he knew when they'd met allowed them just enough time to put down the intended riot before it even had a chance to begin. Flawless. Unheard of. But that's what happened.

George was beside himself. What the hell just happened? Where's Big Ed? If he ratted me out, he's a dead man. Good luck with that, George! And with nary another word, George and his buddies were thrown in the hole. Their kingdom had indeed collapsed and they still didn't know what hit them.

Mikey had won. This round at least. It's amazing how fast news travels, but when they left the prison barely two hours after their entry, a cheer went up from among the inmates. They may not have won their freedom, but freedom had nonetheless won the day. And they would all be the benefactors.

Big Ed was now in a "safe" facility. George and his boys were in solitary confinement twenty three hours per day for several days while the system was properly rebooted. All known leaks were now plugged, and a couple of senior staff had decided to voluntarily submit their resignations. Now this institution just might have a chance.

THE BIG DAY APPROACHES

FOR SOMETHING THAT was supposed to be so important the only people that seemed to be taking it seriously were the wedding planner and the pastor. Trying to meet with the future bride and groom was usually an exercise in futility. But, with only two weeks to go, they realized that maybe they'd better get their act together. So they set it up for tomorrow night at seven. We will be there. Guaranteed!

And they would be, but not before the two of them sat down for what would turn out to be a very long, tumultuous evening. An evening that saw them break up, make up, kiss up, suck up, and any other up you want to throw in there. But they fought through every impasse that threatened to deep six the relationship.

They both wanted this relationship. But the infamous notebook had exposed a tiny crack in their relationship that had morphed into a fracture. Derek couldn't believe that his future wife would willingly put herself in mortal danger just for a story. She, on the other hand, couldn't believe that he was such an old fuddy duddy. She'd never seen this side of him before. Crap, he was acting like an old man.

Truth is, he wasn't. Truth is, she was acting like a bully. Further disclosure: she even scared herself when she got like this. How many times had her boss called her on the carpet for this exact thing? She could hear the tape playing over and over. "Your life is more important than the story." He said it. He meant it. And his business was selling papers. Of course he wanted the story! But he also wanted her around tomorrow. Got it Claire?

Finally Claire backed down. She knew she hurt Derek with her snide remarks. And she knew it was wrong. Even more, she knew he was right. "Baby, I'm sorry. I just get so carried away. I can't stand it when these sleezebags get away with murder. I just want to bury them!"

"Honey, I understand that completely. Why do you think I do what I do. Remember, before you met me I was a homicide detective. I put away bad guys. I still do. But, I don't rush in with guns blazing. The longer I'm around, the more bad guys I can put away. I just want you to be around with me. For a very long time. I don't want to marry you, and a day later, bury you!"

And then they both went silent. She slipped into the crook of his arm and they held each other tightly. "I love you." She whispered into Derek's ear. She could feel the tension leave his body. He held her even more tightly. "Hon, I don't ever want to lose you."

They stayed like that for the longest time. And both vowed to never speak like that to the other again.

Tomorrow night they'd show up for the rehearsal. Hell or high water!

The rehearsal went off without a hitch. It was a small wedding held in the courtyard just outside the church. Perhaps twenty guests at most if they all showed up. These two liked keeping their private life private. They gave away far to much of their lives as it was.

And finally the wedding day arrived! Mikey was nervous, probably more so than the bride and groom. He'd rehearsed this a thousand times. The last thing he wanted was a screwup! "My baby sister! I never could have dreamed this in a million years. Me marrying her!" He looked good. The suit was perfect;the shirt whiter than white; the tie, a deep bold red; shoes that were perfectly polished, and a muscular body that pulled it all together.

It was time. Mikey strode to the front, turned and faced the guests. Derek took his queue and moved to his assigned spot, turning slightly to face the guests. Janice served as the maid of honour. She made her way slowly up the aisle between the rows of guests. Several guests gasped when she'd made her entrance, none more so than Mikey. "My God." To himself. "She's beautiful!" Indeed she was. Derek was hesitant about including Janice in the ceremony, but dared say nothing. He was learning real fast, and as it turned out, that was a very wise decision.

Claire made her way down that very same aisle, her Dad by her side, as the singing of an angel pledging her undying love filled the air. Derek gasped as Claire approached, breaking into a smile as tears uncontained rolled down his cheeks. He didn't care. That was his bride!

She wore traditional white, simple but elegant with just enough cleavage to be enticing. Her auburn hair fell gracefully over her shoulders in a stylish cut that accentuated her Italian heritage. She, too, was an absolute beauty. Derek could not stop shaking his head. Their eyes met, and she too began to weep ever so silently.

At long last these two would become one. Mikey kept it simple. Their request, and much to his relief. They exchanged vows. They exchanged rings. Joline's angelic voice filled the air. It felt as if God himself and stepped into that courtyard for a moment. It was perfect!

And then it wasn't! They all heard the shot. And then all hell broke loose! Derek noticed it first. Mikey's shirt was turning red before his very eyes. He grabbed for his side and fell over backwards before Derek could reach him. "Shooter! Run!"

Claire ran alright. Straight to her brother. "Mikey! Mikey! Can you hear me? Mikey!" He tried to nod. Claire pressed her now soiled wedding dress onto the gaping hole on Mikey's side. The paramedics and police were already on their way. Derek scanned the scattering crowd. Nothing. One shot. Gone. A professional.

The paramedics arrived within minutes. Mikey would be fine. A flesh wound. Like in the movies. Not quite. It hurt like hell! "Can we ask you a few questions?" "For God's sake, can't you do that later?" "Of course." But Derek wasn't about to let the moment pass. "Mikey, did you see anything?" "Nothing man." "Did someone threaten you?" "Just the usual stuff." Ok, let us through." Paramedics put up with a lot of crap. From the good guys as well as the bad guys.

Mikey was on his way to the hospital. The guests were more than willing to call it a day. Thank you very much. The old folks definitely needed a rest after this so off they went. Unknown to Derek and Claire, Janice had jumped in the ambulance to accompany Mikey to the hospital. Joline knew there wasn't a whole lot she could do so she bid her farewell and headed down to the local pub for a brew. Why not? "Certainly the most interesting wedding I've ever been to." Under her breath.

That left the newly married couple. Or did it? They had managed to exchange vows. But, they hadn't signed the official papers yet. That's what they were about to do when the shooting started. Interesting. "Well mister, what now?" "Well, Mrs, how about a drink?" And that's what they did. Blood soaked clothes and all! And since they had picked the same place as Joline, they decided they might as well have a toast or two. Joline, quite eloquently, served as master of ceremonies.

And that's when they heard from Janice. They'd practically forgot about her. "Janice, where are you? Come join us for a drink. It's our wedding you know." And she began to laugh into the phone. "Smarten up! This is serious." Janice was clearly steamed. " I thought you'd be interested in knowing that Mikey's going to be ok. They called it a thru and thru. He'll be in the hospital for a couple of days. They just gave him a sedative to help him sleep. Thought I'd let you know since you're obviously occupied elsewhere." Then she paused. "I'm sorry. I didn't mean to be rude. I'm just upset. Congratulations, by the way."

"You're at the hospital?"

"Yes, I jumped in the ambulance with Mikey. Someone had to."

"Wow! Thank you! We didn't abandon him, you know. The cops wouldn't let us leave without a statement. We knew Mikey was in safe hands. We were just waiting for a call from the hospital and then we were heading up there. Are you still there?"

"Yes. Mikey's sleeping so there's no use me hanging around here. Plus, they have a cop guarding his room. I guess I'll head home."

"No, wait. Come join us. I'll text you the address. There's nothing else we can do tonight anyway. Please! Joline's here. Please come?"

And that's all it took. Janice would join them shortly; just as soon as she checked on Mikey one last time.

Claire hung up the phone. The three of them looked at each other and shrugged. What had just happened? Janice sounded like the Janice of old. They noticed it the moment she made her way up the aisle. And now she was with Mikey making sure he was okay. "I wonder what she'll be like when she gets here?" Fair question.

THE BULLET WAS MEANT FOR . . . WHO?

"**D**EREK, YOU NEED TO see this." He'd been summoned down to headquarters. They had something to show him. "What's up?" "You need to see this." They rolled the video. "Check this out." They ran it three times. Derek sank back into his chair. "Are you seeing what we're seeing?" He was. "Oh my God! Mikey wasn't the target, was he?" They shook their heads in the negative. "Oh my God!"

The video didn't lie. There was nothing ambiguous about it whatsoever. Had Claire not bent over at the exact time that she did to scoop up the flower that had fallen from her bouquet, it would've been her lying there, not Mikey. And she would've been dead. Based on their computer model, and where the bullet had struck Mikey, had it been Claire, it would have went straight through her heart. No question.

"My wife would've been killed on our wedding day. At our wedding. And now I have to tell her that. Oh my God! She's in danger. I've got to go!"

"Hold it. We already have Claire under surveillance. As soon as we saw this. We couldn't wait. Derek, we need to talk to Claire now. It's important."

Of course it was. "I'll go get her now." And then to himself. "Holly crap, what am I going to tell her? See, I was right all along. Oh yeah, that'll go over well! Crap!"

"And we still have to sign papers. Geez!"

CLAIRE, WE NEED TO TALK

S HE WAS A STRAIGHT SHOOTER. He was too. "Claire, you were the target. Not Mikey."

"What? What're you saying? Derek, tell me." She grabbed him by the wrists. "Tell me."

"I'm trying to. I just came from the station. They have the video. Claire, if you hadn't bent over to pick up that stupid flower, you'd be dead right now. It's true. I saw it with my own eyes."

And now it was Claire's turn to slump into the nearby chair. "Oh my God. I knew I was getting close to exposing him. I thought I was safe. Oh my God, Derek, I'm so sorry!" Derek bit his lip. He wanted to yell. He wanted to curse. But he didn't. They were in this thing together. Besides, they were husband and wife. Remember?

"Let's go."

She nodded in agreement. As they got ready to head out the door, Claire beckoned Derek. There's a van parked up the street. It's been there for the past hour. I didn't pay that much attention to it but now I'm wondering." He stopped her there. "That's one of ours. They put a security detail on you the moment they saw the video. Just in case."

Claire told them everything she knew, at least most of it. She left out a couple of details that wouldn't be pertinent to the case. They wouldn't need that. Besides, she still had a story to tell. And now, with this attempt on her life, the story was sure to be a biggie. She could hardly contain her glee. Oops, she'd better temper it down.

After explaining the science of it thoroughly to Claire, all she could think of was how lucky Mikey had been. If he would've been shorter . . . and of course, if she hadn't dropped the flower . . . they were both pretty darn lucky in her opinion. Like luck had anything to do with it!

And now it was time to visit Mikey. "Can we go now, please?" Was she even taking this seriously? "Go ahead but be careful. We'll leave the security detail on for a couple of days." "K, thanks." and off they went.

"Is that woman for real? Rhetorical question, right? I don't think I'd want her after me. And Derek just married her! Good luck, you're gonna need it!"

Derek was wondering much the same. She was nonchalant about what had just went down. Doesn't she realize she could have died yesterday? Or that her brother nearly did?

IT WASN'T FOR YOU, MIKEY

"HI GUYS! GOOD TO SEE YOU. Ouch!" When Claire hugged, she didn't hold back.

"Sorry!"

"It's ok. I'm fine. By the way," and he waved some papers in their face, "we gotta sign these to make it official, you know. Gotta make sure you guys are legal." Leave it to Mikey.

"Nurse. I need a witness. It'll just take a moment. Please." And then it was done. "Now you're legally married. You may now kiss your bride!"

"Thank you pastor. I had an envelope for you but in all the commotion, it got lost. Sorry man!"

"Uh huh. If you say so."

"Oh wait a minute. What's this? Go figure. I thought I'd lost it. It's kinda bloody. You sure you want it?"

"Since I wouldn't want to offend the giver by refusing his gift, I guess I'm obliged to accept it. So I will. And the blood? I've seen plenty of that before. No problem." They all got a good chuckle over that and then it was time to go.

"Whoa. Before you go I have something to ask you. Isn't it kind of strange that the cops aren't asking me more questions? I mean, someone tried to kill me and they're acting like nothing happened. This hole in my side is real, you know."

"You're right. They didn't tell you anything because I told them that we'd handle it."

"Handle what?" Mikey was totally perplexed.

"Mikey, you weren't the target. Claire was."

"What?" gasped Mikey. "Claire. What'd she do?"

Derek wanted to say "don't ask" but he didn't. Not a good idea.

That's when Claire chimed in. " I'm involved in several undercover investigations for my paper. I've gotten too close to the hornets' nest and made some people real nervous. Beyond nervous, obviously."

"Then why did they shoot me?"

So they told him the whole story, and since Derek had copied the video, he got the movie version as well. He was stunned at what they were telling him. "Now what?" was all he could muster. "Now what?"

Now what indeed. They couldn't help but notice that Mikey kept casting his eyes towards the door. "Are you waiting for someone? You keep looking over there." Mikey was about to reply when Janice walked in.

"Sorry, I didn't know you had company. I can come back."

"Janice, get back here." Claire was having none of that. "Hi, it's us. Your family. Come in for God's sake!"

Janice did so somewhat reluctantly. "Hi Mike. Derek. Claire."

Mike piped up. "Glad you made it. I feel better already." And with that, Derek and Claire made their leave. "We'll talk later." To no one who was listening.

"Do you think those two are . . . I don't know. Close? I didn't see that coming."

Derek. "They probably didn't either. It's not like someone gets shot every day, you know."

They knew they were having a weird conversation. And the person they thought was weird, wasn't acting weird anymore, and the pastor wasn't acting very pastoral back there, was he? Just let it go. We have enough to deal with as it is. That was one thing they could agree on!

ALONG CAME JANICE

"THANKS FOR COMING."

"I brought you a Starbucks coffee. I think I got it right. You'd tell me wouldn't you? You're a pastor, so you gotta tell the truth."

"Now, would I lie to you?" He quipped.

Not to be out done. "Would you?"

"It's perfect." he wanted to add "so are you" but he didn't have enough nerve.

And that's how it went for these two. They kidded each other, obviously enjoying the other's company. When it was time for Mikey to leave the hospital, Janice insisted that she take him home. "Sorry O'Malley. But she's way better looking than you. Thanks anyway." O'Malley pretended to be hurt, but he was anything but. "That's my boy!" He chuckled to himself.

JANICE RE-EMERGES

JUST WHEN IT SEEMED that Janice was headed down a one way street the wrong way, she suddenly found an exit that led her to an entry point that allowed her to safely join the flow of traffic headed in the right direction. How she had managed to pull that off was anyone's guess. Janice would later tell those who actually cared, that she was even closer to the abyss than even they had thought.

But for now, she'd appreciate their support, and especially their silence, if or when her name came up. She would tell her story at the appropriate time to the world at large. "Yes, I'm writing a book about my life, but please, don't breath a word about it to anyone. I wasn't even going to tell you, but with recent events, I had no choice. Sorry if I excluded you."

Claire was the first to apologize. "Sis, I'm so sorry. I was . . . we were all so scared for you. And then you shut us out. We thought we'd lost you."

"I was lost. Really lost for awhile. So I don't really blame you, but I kept thinking you guys were going to gang up on me and send me to an institution. Families do that you know!"

The silence in the room was deafening. There were just the four of them, and three of them were feeling downright guilty. To say they hadn't thought exactly what Janice had just stated, would be a bald faced lie. And she knew it.

"Mom, I'm so sorry! We didn't know what to do. We thought we were going to lose you. I'm so glad you're back! I missed you so much!"

And with that she wrapped her arms around her Mom. Claire soon joined in while Derek decided he felt guilty enough staying right where he was. Still, he couldn't figure out how she could have changed so much in such a short amount of time.

"I hope you don't mind, but I've got to go." And with that she stood up, threw her purse over her arm, and began heading for the door.

"Already? Come on. Stay a little longer."

"Can't. Sorry. Gotta go. Bye." And she left them there staring at her departing figure. To herself. "Let's keep them guessing a little longer." And she giggled to herself.

Even Derek couldn't let this pass. "I think I should put a tail on her." Claire piped up. "I'm an investigative reporter. I'll get right on it." Joline threw in her two bits. "And I'll go through her stuff when she's not looking." And that's when they all burst out laughing. "She's back!" In unison.

Was she ever. And she had a date tonight, and nothing was going to interfere with that. Nothing and no one, guaranteed. Even she was shocked. After Jason, she was convinced she would stay single forever. In fact, she wasn't even sure she wanted to talk to another man, except her dad of course. He's different. Of course he is, dear child. He's your dad.

Janice wasn't the only one excited about this evening. He had to admit he didn't have a lot of experience with women, but so what? She seemed to like him, and he was over his head for her! And he was scared.

O'Malley watched all this from a distance. If Mikey only knew how often women were checking him out! But he didn't. Just as well. Besides, Claire's sister had taken a shining to him, and from what he could see, she was a keeper! So he cheered him on from the sidelines. His only advice. "Just be yourself. Take it slow. Let her do the talking. And, breathe. That's all the advice you need from me."

MIKEY GOES TO JAIL

ABOUT SIX WEEKS AFTER the shooting, Mikey had had enough. "Can I please get back to work? This is driving me nuts!" Absolutely. Go for it! And that's what he did.

Two days later, Mikey, along with the previous guests, were on their way back to the prison. This should be most interesting. Of course, Big Ed was gone, and since the hoopla of the previous meeting, George had been sent to another institution where his one hour per day could be spent talking to the ocean. And it seems the prison had decided to replace their Warden for undisclosed reasons. Medical, I believe.

Mikey took a deep breath. A lot had happened since their last visit. Hell, he'd been shot. I guess that would qualify. He wondered how the story had played out in here. They no doubt knew about it.

And did they. This would be an open forum. Questions would be encouraged. But they got way more than they expected. When the guests emerged the packed house erupted . . . in applause. Unheard of! For Mikey.

It seems the story that had made it back to the prison went this way: Mikey had stood up for them. Pissed off the Bosses and got shot as a result. Yet, here he was. As large as life. And he was here to help them! A real stand up guy!

And no one was about to tell them anything different. Mikey had their respect, most of them, a long time before he ever got out of the joint, but this? Hell, that even converted the unconverted. Bring on any program you want, we're in!

When they left the prison that afternoon, they knew they'd scored a major victory. Someone would eventually emerge within the prison and try and establish a pipeline. They would succeed, at least to a degree, but this prison was determined to become a model for reform of a group of inmates the world had thrown away.

From Mikey's point of view it was simple. They may never walk in freedom among those on the outside, but they could live in freedom from the bondage of their sins. God was here. They just needed to knock and He would open the door to a freedom they could have for eternity.

JANICE UNCOVERED

TO SAY THAT JANICE had been shattered by Jason's confession was a huge understatement. It went far beyond that. Even her faith, the rock which she had built her entire life on, was thrown into question. How could a loving God let this happen? In fact, how could He let all the terrible things happening in the world continue? Millions of people were starving to death daily around the world. Abuse of every unimaginable kind took place daily. And a thousand other atrocities were committed in the name of God every day around the globe. What kind of God would allow this? Certainly not a loving, compassionate, caring God. Certainly not the God of the Bible she had grown up with! And to top it off, He let her marry a serial killer? She had stood on her faith her entire life. But it was quickly proving to be nothing but a stack of cards. Don't even bring it up!

It wasn't like she'd never thought about this before. In fact, she had studied it thoroughly and she knew why things are the way they are. She could live with that. At the time she was convinced of the accuracy of the Bible, and she accepted that. She didn't have to like it, but until Jesus returns things would get much worse before they finally got better.

But this was different. Of course it wasn't, but when it's up close and personal, it's like a personal slap from God. Don't bother me. You're not that important to me. Who do you think you are to dare question Me? Like that.

So she walked away. Her parents pleaded with her. So did her Pastor, but to no avail. "Don't ever speak to me about God again!" And that's when she began to lose it. Her grief was real. Her love for Jason was real, despite their differences. Her guilt? Through the roof! How could she have not known? She asked herself that a thousand times over, and then a thousand more.

She began to sleep all hours of the day and night. Nightmares became her friends. Finally, fearing for her very life, Joline was able to convince her to see a psychiatrist, albeit reluctantly. "Now you think I'm crazy, don't you? Ok. I'll show you!" Hey, if that's what it took.

She did go. It was good to vent. She had to concede that much. And she did agree to be medicated. At least the nightmares stopped; well, some of them. But she kept seeing Jason. "Come visit me Janice. I miss you." That never stopped. That's when she made her first visit to the graveyard. Nothing happened while she was there, but each night the same scenario would take place. That's when she decided she needed to dig deeper. And that's when she made the call.

She dared not tell her family, or anyone else for that matter, what she was up to. They would have committed her for sure. The appointment was for seven o'clock this very night. She had arrived early. She wanted to check out the house and anyone coming or going from said residence. She nearly drove away on several occasions but finally steeled herself to follow through. Besides, what could it hurt? As long as she didn't run into anyone she knew, no one would be the wiser. And it wasn't that expensive anyway. Besides, it's my money. She wondered why she'd even said that, even if it was just to herself.

And with that, she took a deep breath and strode across the street into a completely different world. She called herself a practitioner. She'd being done this for over thirty years. She was not a charlatan, but of course you understand, it's difficult to provide references. Confidentiality is ensured.

So Janice was introduced to her first seance. My God, if my family could see me now! She gave her head a quick shake and let the medium be her guide. She was freaked out, no doubt about it, but the smooth voice of the practitioner soon settled her down. "Now we can begin. Just relax and listen to my voice."

The calming voice settled Janice down and she soon forgot where she was. It felt so good, and then the medium spoke. "Jason, are you here?"

Nothing.

"Jason, if you're here, please let us know." Janice was starting to freak out. *My God, what if he actually answered?*

Suddenly the candle flickered. Janice jumped. The medium calmed her down ever so gently. "Jason, is that you?"

"Yes. Ok. I'll tell her." And then to Janice. "He's here. He says Hi. He says he misses you, and that he never meant to hurt you."

Janice recoiled involuntarily and let out a deep gasp. "He's here?"

"Yes. He says you can ask him whatever you want. He can't stay long."

Janice was taken aback. Her hair stood up on the back of her neck. She shivered as if chilled. *Was this real? Oh my God, was this actually happening?*

But she'd better say something. "Ask him why he killed all those people. Why Jason? I want to know why." She began to weep.

"He says he had no choice. He was being controlled by a demon. He never wanted to kill anyone. He wants you to forgive him. He can't rest until you do. I'm losing him. Jason, are you still there?" But he was gone. "I'm sorry. I can't control the other side. All I can do is reach out to them. But now that we've made contact, it'll be far easier the next time. Or at least, that's been my experience." And that was that.

Janice left the home in stunned silence. *Did that really happen? How do I know it's not all made up? And yet, she knew details about Jason and me that no one knew. Is it possible? I must've thought so or what the hell was I doing here?* And these thoughts would consume Janice for the rest of the night.

I'VE GOT THE STORY

S O WHAT IF I COULD'VE been killed? I wasn't, was I? And what a story! Claire was beside herself. This was even better than she could have imaged. And this was just the first piece of scum to fall! There would be others. She had to laugh. Those named in the notebook knew they were there. But what they didn't know was who had the book. All they knew for sure was that the "madam," to put it politely, had brokered a deal and was supposedly on her way to deliver it to the highest bidder when she was murdered. Whoever had murdered her was obviously in possession of said book and it appeared they were intent on taking everyone down. One at a time.

When the article was published and the judges name was there for all the world to see, all hell had broken lose. And that's when it became apparent to the others that they were next in line.

Rumour had it, and it was probably accurate, that the judge had put a hit out on the reporter who had exposed him in the first place. But even that got screwed up. On her wedding day, no less. Talk about keeping things low profile!

It seemed all that did was antagonize the situation, and again, if rumour could be believed, she was coming after him big time. And boy, did she get him! Claire's sentiments exactly. "Gotcha!" And she laughed out loud. "That'll teach you to try and kill me!"

Derek was not happy. Claire was out of control. She thought herself invincible. Even her boss was concerned, and with good reason.

"Claire, take a break. Just for a couple of weeks. Come on. This is crazy." At least he could talk to her like that.

Try being her husband. "Who the hell are you?" But the walls refused to answer. "I want my wife back!"

Short answer. It wasn't going to happen. She wasn't coming back. At least not yet. She had struck the mother lode and she wasn't about to share it with anyone.

"Derek, back off. It's my job. You knew that going in. I can't just up and quit!" And with that she would storm away. "I'm going out!" End of story.

And this is the path she'd continue down for the next two years. There would be numerous death threats but nothing seemed to deter her. She cared little what anyone thought, including Derek. Why had she even bothered to marry? "He knew what he was getting into. Don't blame me! In fact, you can all quit blaming me!"

Derek had bitten his tongue far too many times these past couple of years. In fact, he'd pretty much given up on their marriage. She certainly had. So when Millie asked him to join her for coffee after work one evening, he agreed. Claire was off chasing bad guys anyway, like she cared what he was up to anyways.

And that coffee turned into an evening like he hadn't experienced in over two years. They just talked. But it was fun. He couldn't remember the last time he'd laughed like he did this night. He couldn't help thinking to himself. "This is what I thought we had." And with that thought, he realized that he shouldn't be here. This was not good. He started to interrupt Millie, and then he stopped. "The hell with it. I'm not doing anything wrong." Now convinced, he settled down for another hour before reluctantly making his way home to what he knew would be an empty bed. "This sucks!" And with that, he called it a night.

He awoke with a start. "Hey sleepyhead. Come on. I made breakfast. Your favourite." Claire was back.

"Groggily. "I never heard you come in. Hi." Quick peck on the cheek. "You made breakfast?" "Wow. When was the last time that happened?" Again to himself.

Claire was her usual self. It was as nothing had ever happened. Or that they hadn't seen each other for over a week, or even spoken, for that matter. "I missed you." She crawled onto his knees and gave him a kiss that sent them off into the next room post-haste. That made him late for work, but so what? It wasn't like he didn't bring his work home with him nearly every flippin' day! Wow! Defensive or what?

And of course that's when Claire let him know that she'd be in Houston for the next week. "I have to fly out this afternoon. We're putting the final touches on a huge spread we're running next week. There's never enough hours in the day!"

Derek was happy. For about an hour anyway. Why the hell didn't she just go to Houston in the first place? This stop over to shower and change her clothes was wearing rather thin. Except for the post-haste thing, they might as well have been room mates! "Ok, hon. I gotta get to work. Call me when you get to Houston, ok?" And with that, he headed out the door. "Huh." He shrugged. "Whatever."

Millie greeted him the moment he walked through the door. "Morning sleepyhead."

"Morning." Sorry, Claire showed up this morning. She's heading to Houston this afternoon. I thought I'd better introduce myself to her before she forgot who I was." He shook his head. Millie stared but wisely said nothing. "Poor guy." Under her breath.

So Claire did as Derek had so snidely alluded to. Except that she decided a bubble bath was in order, not a shower, thank you very much. Add in a few changes of clothes and she would be set for the next week. Life was good! Oh, perhaps she should throw in that hot little number just in case. Why not?

To herself. "I'm so lucky to have Derek. He's so understanding. Sometimes I don't know how he does it. He's a keeper!" And off she went back into her alternate universe.

Derek knew her plane was leaving at two. At two ten, he breathed a sigh of relief. "Good. She's gone." And that's when he caught himself. "Oh my God!" He thought back to a time, not that long ago, when he would've gave anything for her to give up that life, and never leave his side. And now. Whatever.

IT'S ALWAYS DARKEST BEFORE THE DAWN

T O SAY JANICE WAS IN a dark place would be an understatement. That first visit to the practitioner had really done a number on her. "Was that really Jason?" How was that possible? And I never heard him speak. Just the medium. It was probably all fake. But how did she know so much about us? I didn't tell her. Oh my God! This is crazy!"

Crazy or not, it led Janice into the world of the occult. She would resist as best she could, but only for two or three days at a time, and then she'd make another visit. Money changed hands but that didn't really bother her. But she wasn't getting the relief from these sessions that she thought she might, and that confused her. If anything, it was drawing her closer to the abyss. If something didn't happen soon, she knew she'd soon be joining Jason. And where that might have had some appeal earlier, that was dissipating with each subsequent visit.

Her family thought she was going crazy. She thought she was as well. But then one night after another session, she did something she never thought she'd ever do again. It was about 9:30 when she drove past the church. On impulse, she turned around and parked across the street from the church she'd attended since a youth. A flood of memories enveloped her as the tears began streaming down her face. "How I loved this place. God. I know you're real. I know it's not your fault.

I need you. I'm so scared!" What had been tears only moments ago became a stream she could not contain.

That's when she heard the knock. Startled, she looked up to find her pastor tapping on her window. She quickly wiped her eyes and rolled down the window. "Janice, come in. Please. Let's talk." That was it. She spoke not a word as he led her into the sanctuary and to the front. Up to that beautiful cross that she'd admired since a child. She could no longer hold back the tears. He held her as he might a child, and she cried unabashedly for what seemed an eternity. And finally, they were able to talk. At midnight, Janice drove home. And then she slept until noon the next day.

When she finally arose, she did so with a smile on her face. Not a single nightmare last night! It may be darkest before the dawn but Janice's darkness had broken late last night, in that sanctuary in front of that cross, wrapped in the arms of Jesus himself. Ok, Jesus' representative.

CLAIRE TAKES HOUSTON

"I LOVE MY LIFE!" Claire knew she had another one in the bag. The story. She had to laugh. "The way it's going, I'll be competing with myself for the story of the year." No conceit here.

But it was true that she was taking them down, one at a time. Mercilessly, like they'd do to her if they ever got their hands on her. She wasn't about to let that happen anytime soon if she had anything to say about it. The best way she could stay alive was to remain as high profile as possible and get as much dirt on these scumbags as she could. And make sure that they knew she had copies held in very safe places. She'd deal. She wasn't shy about losing files on some low life if it gave her access to someone higher up the food chain. And probably saved a few families along the way, that is, until they returned to their low life ways, and set them selves up for someone like her to take them down again. Once a criminal . . . almost always, a criminal. Claire'd seen it a thousand times.

Still, she knew she lived a precarious life. She should never have gotten married. What was she thinking? How many times had she asked herself that question? And when she actually got her mind off herself, she realized how much crap she'd put Derek through. And still was. "I wouldn't blame him if he told me to take a hike."

DEREK THE LOST

D EREK HAD BEEN IN a few relationships, but even at their worst, they were better than what he had now. Married, but no wife. Obviously her work was a whole lot more important than him. That made him feel real good. "Thanks Claire." Under his breath.

As usual he was the last to leave. Go where? That never used to bother him all that much, but that was before he had someone in his life. And now. Well, he had done it voluntarily. He was about to switch off the lights when she spoke. "Derek."

"Millie? Why're you still here? Everyone's gone."

"I thought you might want to talk. Maybe grab a coffee or something."

"I'm not very good company right now, I'm afraid. It's not been a very good day."

Millie wasn't about to give up that easily. "Tell you what. Why don't we order in a pizza or something and chat right here? How about that?"

"That would work. I just don't feel like being out in public. I might bite someone's head off. Are you sure you want to be around me?"

"I'll order." Done. If he didn't want to talk, that was fine with her. Besides, if she wasn't doing this, she'd be heading home to an empty apartment anyway. "I can't believe Claire would leave this guy alone for any reason, let alone a story. She's crazy!"

She'd ordered a six pack to go along with the pizza. Before long, Derek had loosened up and they settled back into the banter of a couple of nights ago. Conversation with Millie was so easy. It was like they'd known each other forever. Derek began to wish . . . and then he stopped. "Wow. What am I doing? This is wrong." And after a moments hesitation, he cracked another beer.

Millie was not a drinker. After two beer she was flying high and loving every minute of it. Derek's mood had changed dramatically, and soon they were attempting to do a two step to the old time music blaring from the antique radio that must have came over on the Mayflower.

It was inevitable. That first kiss. They both wanted it. They both knew it. And all it took was a little liquid courage, and that had made the trip with the pizza.

Now what? They both apologized to the other but neither one would pull away. They didn't apologize for the second kiss. Or the tenth. Or . . . "They took separate cabs home that night. It seemed like the appropriate thing to do. Both had a lot to think about. And so did Claire.

PUT ON YOUR BIG GIRL PANTS

C LAIRE MAY HAVE TAKEN her mind off herself on occasion, especially when it came to Derek. She really did feel bad for him. But, she always reminded herself, he knew what he was getting into. I guess if one says that enough, eventually one believes it. She did. But, soon she was all about Claire once more.

She was more agitated than usual this evening. She'd flown in early fully expecting to meet with a potential eyewitness that could shed some light on a particularly vulnerable case she'd been working on. And now, he'd cancelled until the next evening.

She had nothing else scheduled beyond that interview, and pacing up and down the confines of her hotel room was wearing thin rather quickly. "To hell with it. I need a drink." And with that she headed downstairs to the lounge. She wasn't a big drinker but a couple of glasses of wine might just take the edge off.

And it did, but by the third, she was heading into unwise territory. Rarely is there an upside when one begins to lose one's way. Of course, there are always those standing by ready to help. Often the question becomes: ready to help whom exactly? The answer is often: to help themselves, who else? Do you really think I'm here to help you?

Claire was no one's fool, but that extra glass of red had really done a number on her. And that nice gentleman was more than willing to help. So she accepted his help. She thought nothing of it when he suggested that perhaps they get another patron to assist them in getting her to her room.

They made their way to the elevator and eventually to her room on the 20th floor. "Thank you so much. True gentlemen. I can take it from here." Thru slurred words which convinced the "gentlemen" to escort her inside the suite, instead of just to the door.

She protested but ever so slightly. "We're going to go now, Ok? We'll make sure the doors locked behind us. Night." And they were gone. Claire ran a bath, settled in, and only then did it occur to her how vulnerable of a position she'd put herself in. "Oh my God, Claire. What the hell!" Claire was not one to let down her guard. Ever. And yet she had. Had they wanted to do whatever, and she shuddered, there wouldn't have been a damn thing she could have done about it! "That will never happen again!"

She lounged in the tub until the chilled water bade her move. She reluctantly towelled herself off and made her way to the bed. It wrapped her in its arms until the night gave way to the dawn. She awoke and stretched as might a feline, and slowly extracted herself from the comfort of the down filled delight that surrounded her. A quick dart to the shower and soon Claire would return to the world of today.

She took her time. Hair, makeup, appropriate clothes for the office would fit the bill. Her boss was expecting her around eleven. A nice leisurely breakfast would be the perfect end to a beautiful morning. And then she involuntarily shuddered. "I nearly blew it last night. Never again."

So Claire had gotten away with her lapse in judgment the previous evening. Even more bizarre was that she would even put herself into a compromising situation considering the fact that she was enemy #1 on more than one hit list."Claire." She admonished herself. "That's how reporters end up being the story, not telling the story!"

So she set about gathering her laptop and the accompanying notebooks, etc. which accompanied her everywhere. No exceptions. This was her life's work and it wasn't going anywhere except with her. Even on the plane. Carry on only.

"Strange." To herself. "Where's the witness file I was working on last night? I must've stuck it in another file. Where are you?" She always talked to herself. But it wasn't to be found. And then she knew.

She slowly slumped into the oversize chair just waiting to envelope her. "Oh my God! What've I done?" But she knew.

The thing is, she could've been dead. Instead, they just took the file. Had she resisted, the ending might have already been written for her. But because of her stupidity, the ending for the witness was all but assured. There would be no going back from a mistake of this magnitude. Her boss knew she had the file. In fact, she was supposed to have cemented it the previous night had the witness not cancelled. She hadn't bothered to inform her boss of the change in plans; she was seeing him this morning anyway. She'd tell him then. Besides, the interview had been rescheduled for tonight anyway. Now all hell would break loose!

And it did. In spades. Our star reporter. Duped by her own stupidity! And her boss was not about to hold anything back. She did not suffer fools gladly, and she was about to find out that neither did he. They may have been friends, but he was also her boss, and Claire had pushed way to many buttons, way too many times. Enough was enough! The Claire that had walked into his office moments ago was not the same Claire that emerged.

She had few friends at the paper. The log in her eye had distorted her vision long ago, and where she was once revered, and a friend to everyone, she was now reviled. "Get out of our face! We don't need friends like you!" Not spoken but definitely thought.

So she left the building, hailed a cab and made her way back to her hotel. She had room service deliver her a bottle of their finest red wine. She once again readied the tub while waiting for room service to arrive. There was a knock at the door. It startled her at first. "Who is it?" "Room service." "What do you have for me?" She was not taking any more chances. They answered appropriately. She opened the door to allow entry and quickly whisked them away. Tub time, wine time, thinking time. Her bubble had burst. She could either take her toys and go home or put on her big girl pants. And anyone knowing Claire knew exactly what she'd do!

CONSEQUENCES OF A FILE LOST

LAIRE KNEW WHAT the consequences would be for the witness turned stool pigeon. The papers confirmed it the next day. And for the first time in a very long time, she wept. Not for herself, but for the man who risked his life and that of his family to expose the sordid underbelly of the Jericho Foundation. They cast themselves as an NGO dedicated to the reunification of lost children and their families that had been torn apart by the ravages of war in Latin America. They were US based but it turned out that their "real" business was procuring children for their wealthy clients. Of course, there were many reunifications that took place to divert attention away from their real purpose. One was a zero sum business; the one their sponsors and supporters endorsed; the other was a multimillion dollar enterprise that worked for everyone save the families they were set up to serve. Finally, a mole had made his way to the surface with enough info to put these guys out of business for good. Now, he was dead. And Claire was responsible. At least partially.

But this was far from over. They may have temporarily diverted attention away from themselves but once Pandora's box was opened, even a crack, it was impossible to ever shut it completely again. Claire may have been careless but she wasn't stupid. She always had a backup system in place. Unfortunately, her carelessness had resulted in the death of her mole. He was a husband and a father. He'd screwed up a lot in his life, but he'd finally owned up to it, and was about to undo a whole lot of wrongs with this one act. Now what?

DEREK'S DILEMMA

SLEEP DID NOT COME easy for Derek that night. He'd stepped over a line he never thought he would. And worst of all, he didn't care. To be perfectly honest, he wished they would've taken it further. It had felt so good! Someone wanted to be with him, and he wanted to be with her.

He tried to assess his guilt. But he wasn't feeling particularly guilty. "My God! We haven't even been married a year and I already feel this way. Is this how Claire feels? She must. Crap!"

And on he went. "Maybe it's for the best. Better now than dragging it out and screwing up both our lives. I wonder if she's screwed around on me? Funny. Maybe I'm just too trusting." And on he babbled.

He was doing his best to justify his actions of the previous night and doing a pretty good job of it. "How do I know what Claire's up to? She's gone more nights than she's here, and it's always "undercover," whatever that means." Keep going Derek. You should have yourself convinced pretty soon. Blame her for something else. Whatever it takes to justify your own actions. Don't forget how she keeps telling you that "you knew what you were getting into." Use that one, Derek.

Derek had pretty much convinced himself that Claire had probably done a whole lot more than he ever had. "She's the one with the secrets, not me. God, I'm so naive!"

And that's when the phone rang. Claire? Weird. She always texted. "Hello."

"Hi baby. I just needed to hear your voice." She sounded like she was a million miles away.

"Where are you? Are you ok?"

She began to weep. He could hear her sniffling. It took him aback. "What's wrong, baby?" He gave his head a shake. Just minutes ago, he was convinced that they were done. Over. That's all she wrote. And now. " Hon, talk to me."

She tried. He caught fragments of her words between her sobs. "I'm so sorry. I don't deserve you. Please give me another chance."

What the hell? Did she know about last night? There's no way she coulda known. Still, this was freaking him out.

"Derek, please don't give up on me. Please baby."

This was getting stranger by the minute. "Why would I give up on you?" He didn't know what else to say.

She continued. "Is there any way you could get a couple of days off? I need to be with you. Just the two of us. Please, baby."

"Now? Today?"

"Please baby. Just a couple of days. Please!"

She was not one to beg. What the hell is going on? "I could probably swing it. Tomorrow would work a lot better. At least that would give me time to line someone up to handle my files. Will that work?"

"I wish you could come today. Maybe tonight? After work?" She sounded totally desperate.

He'd never heard her sound like this. He needed to go. Now. "I'll see what I can do and call you back shortly. You want me to meet you in Houston, right?"

She answered in the affirmative. "I know it sounds strange, but I have to be here for the next few days. I can't wait to see you."

"Ok, I'll call you in a bit." Crap! This didn't sound good at all. He knew he could get out of work easily enough. Bigger problem. What was he going to tell Millie?

It only took one call to book off for a couple of days. Telling Millie would be quite another matter. She'd made it pretty clear the previous night that she was looking forward to seeing him again this evening. And to make matters even worse, he'd told her exactly the same thing. And now he was about to get on a plane to go see his wife. He was beginning to wonder exactly who he was cheating on. This is nuts!

THE PASTOR'S INTERNS

GETTING SHOT HAD PROVEN to be a blessing in disguise for Mikey and his cohorts. His credibility at the prison had shot up like a rocket. They knew him before. They liked and accepted him. Darn near as much as Charley. But when Mikey stood up to the Big Dog, and then the Boss, and survived being shot, well, he was the man. And they meant that in the best possible way. So what if the bullet hadn't even been meant for Mikey? They didn't need to know that. Besides, everything else they believed was the truth and Mikey was not about to wilt this opportunity pass.

"We need to train up one of the guys to be a Pastor, like Charley was, and then me. Agreed."

The other members of the board nodded their heads in agreement. Since bringing Mikey on board, change after change had been implemented. Even more importantly, the inmates had bought in to the ongoing transformation. They may never get out of prison but life was a lot better now than it was even a few months ago.

Mikey's biggest concern was to ensure the momentum continue. He could make it up to the prison a couple of times per week, which was great, but then it was up to the inmates to police themselves for the next several days until the next visit. That's when it got hairy. Not everyone bought into this pseudo Cinderella story, and they were determined to wrestle their prison back from the hands of this Christian mob. No one dare let their guard down too much less they end up permanently sleeping.

So far the "good guys" were able to hold their own, but it was inevitable that the old pipelines would be reestablished. And once they were, the drugs would flow as before, and a whole bunch of the "good guys" would get swallowed up. Guaranteed!

Having a full time pastor wasn't an absolute guarantee but it gave the outside full time ears, and that was paramount to keeping control of the prison. And it was a lot easier to form their own "gang" to ensure their safety. It's a different life on the inside, and most of these guys would never leave this place. It was theirs. The kind of life they'd have inside this place would depend almost entirely on who was in control. At the end of the day, it'd better be them.

Fortunately, Mikey had been mentoring a couple of the inmates several times weekly while he was still inside. He'd used the same tactic on them as Charley had used on him. They bought into it, and as a result, the two of them were now less than a year away from being ordained. More importantly, they were both big boys, and they had each other's backs. Now it was up to Mikey to bring them up to speed.

Mikey had approached the board with a suggestion that surprised them. "I'm willing to go back inside for a couple of weeks to get the boys oriented properly. It's not that I want to, but I think it makes the most sense. What do you think?"

"Seriously? I'm shocked you even want to go there at all. I sure wouldn't." The board chair was the first to speak. The others nodded in unison. "Mikey, you don't have to do this. I know you love those guys, but you know as well as I do, they'd slit your throat in a minute."

"It's the best way. We've gone as far as we can. We're hanging on but I know these guys, and if they ever get the upper hand, we're screwed. Two weeks. That's all I ask. It's our best shot."

How do you argue with someone willing to put his life on the line for a bunch of lifers? It's not like there were any other's volunteering to take his place. It was a risk, but in Mikey's eyes, it was worth it. Ok, why not? Just pray to God nothing goes wrong!

And that's what happened. Mikey was sent back to jail, albeit by his own volition. That made a whole lot of the inmates very happy, but it pissed off a few others. Ok, buddy, bring it on! You're going down! You shoulda stayed away!

ARE YOU NUTS!!!

WHEN JANICE HEARD what Mikey was up to, she lost it. "Are you out of your mind?"

"Oh oh. Sorry, was I supposed to check with you first?" That's what he thought but he didn't say a word.

But that was ok. She wasn't given him time to answer anyway. "You could be killed, for God's sake! I could see a couple of times a week but now you're going there to live? Do you have a death wish or something?" Janice wasn't about to hold back.

Mikey figured the best thing to say was nothing, but he doubted that would go over very well, so he gave it a shot. "It had to be done. It's the only thing that made any sense. We've put to much work into the prison to lose it now. I had to do it."

Janice had begun to calm down a bit. "I'm sorry I yelled at you,but geez Mikey, you're scaring me. I don't want to lose you too." She could feel her cheeks beginning to burn. Why'd I say that?

Mikey heard it too. She really likes me. I should have asked her for her opinion. Damn!

"It's just for a couple of weeks. Otherwise, everything Charley and I worked for could be lost. I can't do that to Charley. And I'm not going to leave the guys inside stranded. They need me. They're my family." That's it. That's why he had to do this. They were his family. My God, he'd been inside for over thirty years! He shrugged his shoulders. "I gotta do what I gotta do. Sorry."

Janice knew he was right. She also knew they'd kill him without a second thought. She knew a little bit about this subject. And that got her to thinking. "How is it that the two guys I was/am most attracted to are killers. Man, do I have good taste, or what!" She felt guilty the moment the thought escaped, but it was true. She knew Mikey's situation was totally different than Jason's but still . . .

And with that Janice took her leave. "I've got to go. Good luck Mikey. I'd like to say I understand, but I don't. Sorry. Bye." Then she was gone.

Mikey stood staring at the back of the door. And then he called O'Malley. "Can we meet?"

"Of course. Usual place?"

"You bet. See you in twenty."

NO MORE MEN!

J ANICE COULDN'T DRIVE. She'd just left Mikey's place completely flabbergasted at what he'd just committed to. He didn't get it. None of these flippin' men had a clue! That was it. She was done! And finally she'd stopped shaking long enough to start the car. She'd better take it easy. She was still pissed. At him and at the whole lot of them. Good thing he's not out on the road right now. She'd probably run him over! Probably hurt less than someone stabbing you to death!

There was so much more to this than Mikey's decision to go back inside. She knew right then and there that she still had a long ways to go. She'd fooled herself into thinking that she was ready for another relationship. But, she wasn't. She may never be. And the two guys she liked the best. Sorry, Mikey, but you both killed people! What the hell was I thinking? I'd better call the shrink tomorrow. Yeah, that's what I'll do.

It was just as well. She certainly wasn't ready and Mikey barely knew what a woman looked like. Ok, slight exaggeration, but he'd been inside for over thirty years. So, a forty five year old man that had never dated was suddenly cast upon the free world and didn't have a clue what to do. But it wouldn't take long and he'd know more about women that he ever cared to know.

But that would have to wait. He had an appointment at the prison two mornings from now. Somehow, I think that'll be a whole lot easier to deal with than a woman's emotions. "But when I get out, I gotta get this woman thing figured out." Good luck with that!

JOLINE COMES HOME

JANICE HAD DECIDED to hunker down and begin working on the outline of the adult book she was contemplating writing. She wasn't sure if she was ready to expose herself to the world just yet, in fact, she would likely write it under a completely different pen name. She'd probably write it as non fiction and then gently ease it into the fiction category. Somehow that felt safer. Even then, she knew she'd be exposing herself but it would be much easier to deny. It's fiction, after all.

She sat back, studying her outline when the phone rang. She usually shut it off when writing, but she hadn't written in such a long time, she'd completely forgotten to switch it to silent. Just as well. "Hi Mom."

"Joline! Hi baby. I was thinking about calling you tonight. How are you?"

"I'm great! Mom. You remember that I'm leaving on Monday for Paris, right?"

"I remember. Can't you come home for a few days before you go? I hate it when you're so far away. Grandma and Grandpa keep asking me about you."

"Mom. That's why I'm calling. I checked and we can fly directly out of Seattle. I thought Erin and I could stay with you for a few days before we leave. If that's ok with you."

"Yes. Of course. Erin's always welcome her. You know that."

"I know, but you know me. I don't like assuming things. We visited Erin's parents a few days ago. Gotta keep the parents happy, you know!" And she laughed.

"Ok. I'll make up the guest room for Erin. And I'll call grandma and gramps to let them know you're coming. And I'll . . . "

"Mom. Slow down. Relax. We'll be arriving around 3 on Thursday. That gives us lots of time to visit everybody. Can you pick us up or should we catch a cab?"

"I'll pick you up. Should I tell everyone you're coming or . . . ?"

"Don't tell anyone. Friday morning I'll do my usual jog past their place. I bet anything gramps will see me."

And that's how they left it. Janice was beside herself. Joline was always on the go. This trip would take her and Erin to France to begin their trek of the Camino Frances, nearly five hundred miles long. They had been planning this pilgrimage for the past year, and the time had finally arrived. They'd both worked their butts off to ensure they had enough cash to last them for a couple of months.

Janice was so proud of her little girl. Thank God she wasn't going alone. Joline did things like that. Fortunately she'd met Erin on a previous trek and they'd become fast friends. Neither was interested in settling down yet, much to the chagrin of many a young man. There was always time for that later. Much later, hopefully, in Janice's opinion. In any case, she's coming home. And Janice did a little dance right then and there!

DEREK GOES TO HOUSTON

TO SAY HE WAS MORE than a little curious would be an understatement. He'd never heard Claire talk like that before. She was subdued, almost apologetic in her speech, unlike the Claire he knew. Was she going to confess something to him he didn't want to hear? Were they over? And if so, why was she begging him to come? Crap, these and a thousand other questions bombarded him the entire trip. "Relax, Derek." To himself. "Just relax."

He'd called her the moment he'd cleared his schedule to confirm his arrival time. She seemed to be over the moon. "I can't wait to see you." Her words. And yet in the past, he'd always felt dismissed. And now he needed to talk to Millie.

"I'm heading to Houston for a few days. Claire has some function that she wants me to attend with her. Kind of a last minute thing. Sorry, but I had no choice." "Liar!" To himself.

Millie was peed. "That would be just like Janice. She must've sensed something. That woman's a bitch. And you're an idiot!" All under her breath. But instead. "See you when you get back. Have fun."

Derek wasn't expecting that. He thought she'd be peed right off. Instead, she told me to have a good time. "What the hell?" And then. "I'll never understand women!" You're not alone, buddy. You're not alone!

When he knocked on the door he heard her call out. "Who is it?" Cautious. "It's me babe."

The door swung open and Claire enveloped him in the biggest bear hug ever. " I love you, Derek. I love you so much!" Ok. Now he knew something was definitely wrong! "Oh my God, she'd had an affair! What else could it be?" All under his breath. He steeled himself for whatever was to follow. "You can handle this Derek. Be strong." Again to himself.

"I'll pour us a glass of wine. Freshen up if you like." He headed to the bathroom, leaving the door slightly ajar. He could see her pouring the wine, and then she turned up the fireplace a little; dimmed the lights way down low and turned on their favourite music. "Wow. The perfect seduction scene." He thought to himself. "What's going on?"

The atmosphere was set, and any resolve he had coming in, was long gone. He settled in beside her on the chaise and prepared for . . . actually, he didn't know what he was prepared for. "Please let it be good. Please." He talked to himself nearly as much as Claire did.

So she began. But she was no dummy, so she started it off the right way. "Derek, the moment I first met you, I knew I wanted to be with you. But I was stubborn, even back then, and I resisted calling you. For a whole year, remember?" Which he did. She continued. "But I couldn't get you out of my mind. I was so busy trying to prove to the world that I was the best at what I did that I was prepared to throw us away without even giving us a chance. Did you know that?"

"Not really. I knew I liked you but I wasn't sure if you felt the same." He was about to begin rambling when she cut him off. "Sorry babe. I need to get this off my chest." "Oh great. Here it comes." And he steeled himself yet again.

Claire continued. " I thought I had my insecurities under control by the time I called you to meet up in Seattle. I wasn't sure you'd even remember who I was, but of course, you did. And you know what happened then." She paused, and then. "I was absolutely convinced that a move to Seattle was the perfect fit for me. I could be with you, even work with you from time to time, and still do the odd assignment around the country and have a normal life. Ok, not normal, but you know what I mean."

Derek was about to say something but no. She covered his lips with her fingers, gave him a quick peck on the cheek, and carried on. "But then three huge things happened, as you know. Mikey, obviously, and everything that went with that. And then the whole Jason thing and my family, and all the rest of it. And the notebook. That lit a fire that I couldn't control. It drove me crazy." And that's when Claire began to sob, and then the tears began to flow, and the streams became rivers. All he could do was hold her. He said nothing.

Finally, she began again. "And that's when my work became more important to me than you or anyone else. I was consumed. This was the stuff I'd dreamed about as a young reporter. The Big Story! And now I had a bunch of them. I was the queen. I had it made! But I didn't. I did some stupid things. I got other people killed. Derek, it's my fault that people died. I couldn't leave it alone!" And she began to cry again. "And I drove you away. The person I loved most in this world and I drove you away!"

Derek held her even closer. He didn't want her to see the tears streaming down his face. He replayed her words. " the person I loved most in this world." Me, she's talking about me!"

Not another word was spoken for a very long time. Finally, he spoke. "Claire, I've always loved you. I still do. Very, very much." "Sorry, Millie, I love my wife." That part to himself.

They stayed like that for several hours, sipping their wine, listening to the tunes they loved, and enjoying their togetherness. It'd been so long. Intimacy had fled their marriage long ago, but on this night it returned with a vengeance. Both knew they'd have work to do, but both were determined to do whatever was necessary. They had found each other. Then they'd come dangerously close to losing each other forever. But that was yesterday.

JOLINE ARRIVES

FOR A TIME JOLINE thought she'd lost her mother. The whole Jason fiasco had taken her mom to the brink, and for a while, over the brink. Their family had even considered having her committed. For her own safety. And then, almost miraculously, she'd started to recover. Slowly at first, and then in leaps and bounds. And finally she had her Mom back!

But as life became increasingly normal, Joline found herself too contained. She thought she could make Seattle her box, but she couldn't. She needed to fly, and it wasn't going to happen as long as she was here. And now that her Mom was getting well again, it became obvious, even to her grandparents, that she needed to go.

She remembered the discussion she and her Mom had just a few months back. At the time, she wasn't sure how her Mom would react. She should've known better. Her Mom had always supported her decisions and she wasn't about to quit now. So Joline left and followed her dreams. And now she was about to follow another, but she still needed to see her mom first. And Grammy and Gramps.

Joline had always been quite private about her life. Perhaps that was because she was such an active blogger with a substantial following. One never knew if a follower could be a potential stalker or not. It had never happened to her personally, but she knew of cases that had ended very badly. She had no intention of becoming a victim or putting her family in peril. Thus, her social life was one thing; her private life, quite another.

Even bringing home a friend seemed weird at first. But her family wanted to know more about her life. It wasn't like they'd ever accompany her on some of her excursions into the far reaches of the known world. This was a relatively benign journey, albeit a long one, and since she'd be gone for over two months, she'd figured she might as well introduce them to her travelling companion. She'd met Erin's parents on a couple of occasions, and since it turned out that they could fly out of Seattle anyway, she might as well have Erin meet her family.

Janice was beside herself. She'd finally get to meet Erin. Joline had spoken of her on various occasions. It seemed the two of them had crossed paths on numerous travels, and finally decided to do the Camino Frances together. They were sojourners on their own pilgrimages, but they figured they could handle each other for a month or so. Solo travellers do so for their own reasons. They were about to find out if they could handle more than their own company.

"Hi Mom. This is Erin."

Janice hugged her daughter and then she hugged Erin. "I'm so happy to meet you. Joline's told me so much about you!" And she hugged her again.

Joline and Erin exchanged glances. Erin was every bit as private as Joline. "No I didn't." She mouthed the words to Erin.

"Do you mind if we slip by Grammy and Gramps for a minute? They're so excited to see you!"

"Mom. I told you I wanted to surprise them."

"I know. And I tried not to say anything but I was so excited. And you know how Gramps is, and . . . I'm sorry, baby." Oh Janice, Janice.

"It's ok, Mom. Let's stop by. It's fine. Besides, it's too late now. Right?" That's her mom.

So they stopped. Erin loved watching them interact. For a moment she was jealous. " I wish my family was like that."

But if she thought she'd be excluded, she was wrong. "And this is Erin. We've heard so much about you!" But of course they hadn't. Still, she got more hugs in the next two minutes than she'd gotten in, oh my God, forever! "I like these people. Can I move in?" To herself even though she wanted to say it out loud.

Finally, home. "Erin, don't be shy while you're here. My home is your home. Your room is the first one on the right. The bathrooms just across the hall. Use whatever you need. Don't be shy." And with that she gave Erin another hug. "I'm taking you girls out for dinner later. My treat!"

"Mom!" But there was no use protesting. She wouldn't hear it anyway.

The next couple of days sped by, and much to the chagrin of Janice, the girl's had to leave. As usual, a whole pile of hugs were the order of the day, and then they were off. Off to a new adventure. In a new land. And as much as Erin was looking forward to this new adventure with her friend Joline, she wished she could live in the box she was just leaving. If only.

JAIL BIRD ONCE MORE

NOT REALLY. BUT MIKEY wasn't sure about the street clothes. He would've fit in a whole lot better dressed as the inmates were. Anyway. Deal with it. You got your wish, didn't you? He had. If this went sideways, this could be disastrous not only for him, but the entire program. Failure was not an option. It was time to get to it.

It became apparent immediately that he was a marked man. He had his protectors but it was equally obvious that there'd been a hit ordered on him. "Charley, where are you?" Under his breath. He couldn't help but think back to those days so very long ago when Charley had taken him under his wing. He had to chuckle remembering Charley's words: "you're gonna finish your schooling; you're gonna learn the Bible, and you're gonna hit the gym every day; and then he added, don't ever be alone."

But alone he was. Tensions were high. At any moment all hell could break loose, and if it did, he knew who they were coming for. "It's best I get to work." To himself of course. "Ok, guys. We need to talk." At least that was one thing they'd agree to. He could meet with his interns as often as he wished, under the protection of the guards. He had two weeks. He best not waste it.

The interns, Enrico and Robert, had been here for about the same length of time, 7 and 8 years respectively. Both had been nailed for armed robbery; both were serving life sentences. Both had jumped on board early on in their sentences knowing that if they ever expected to taste freedom, they had to get straight, and they had to stay away from the gangs.

The gangs had tried to recruit them. And they'd been threatened more times than they could remember, but they both stuck to their guns. Both knew why they had survived in this world gone mad. And now he was standing before them asking them to follow him once again. And both knew that they would die for Mikey if need be.

He was determined that wouldn't be the outcome. The best way was to recruit some followers, others who would stand up against the onslaught that was sure to come. It always did, and this place would be no exception. Except now it was extremely high profile. The last thing they wanted was attention. Killing Mikey would give them attention they didn't want, but he was an exception, and he had to be brought down. He, singlehandedly, was destroying everything they'd worked for in this joint. He had to go. He was here for two weeks. Plenty of time to get rid of him once and for all.

This was no secret. Nor was it to the guards. Fortunately, the changing of the guards and the warden, as well as the sudden departure of two of their "bosses," had severely weakened the gang structure. Even in a place like this, there were a hell of a lot more "good" guys than "bad," and Mikey fully intended on utilizing that to his advantage.

So they held their meetings. Enrich and Robert were encouraged to lead these groups. Each would be assigned a specific group, but the groups were not to be in competition with the other. They had a common enemy and that's what they'd have to stand firm against.

They say God will find you in your darkest place. That's what he did here. It's so easy for outsiders to sneer at a jailhouse confession or conversion. "They're just saying that so they can get a reduced sentence. They don't mean it." Yeah, right. Easy for them to say. But I'm not sure that God looks at it quite the same way as the pew sitters. "Judge not let he be judged by the same measure." I know I'm not about to judge anyone. Not me.

Mikey knew that the work they were doing was life changing, and in fact, it was life giving. Eternal life. Offered freely to those who would accept the gift. Most of the inmates would never walk the streets again as a free man, but this life was short. The next life offered them eternity, and if the pew sitters had accepted the free gift as most of these inmates had, they may well be walking the streets of gold, hand in hand. All free men.

Mikey knew he could die in here. But he knew it was worth the risk. Enrico and Robert understood the risk as well, but they knew eternity was at stake. And they'd stand in the gap until their dying breath if need be. To say Mikey was proud of these guys would be a gross understatement.

The first week went by with little fanfare. The interns were soaking this stuff up, and prepping themselves up as much as they could before Mikey left. They'd need every bit of wisdom and every prayer they could muster once he was gone. Mikey knew and they knew it. But with each passing day their ranks grew, and other than fearing possible infiltrators, they knew they could handle this. They knew little of Charley but by reputation, and they'd had the good fortune to be mentored by Mikey. They'd be ready. And if there's one thing they knew: Start with prayer instead of using it as a last resort!

JANICE IS BACK

HAVING JOLINE HOME had been a blessing. All was right with the world, well, not really, but she was going with that theme regardless. She couldn't remember when she'd been as happy as she was the past few days. Joline was home; she got to meet Erin; they had spent considerable time with Mom and Dad which was great for everyone; and they'd got to spend a few hours with Derek and Claire. Unfortunately, they'd been out of town and had just returned, but at least they got to visit for a couple of hours.

And now everyone was gone. The silence was deafening. Funny, she used to crave the silence. Easier to write. But now. "Careful Janice." But it was too late. Mikey was on her mind. Damn. She didn't want him there but he chose to show up anyway.

She wasn't really mad at him. But she was scared for him. And rightly so. He'd treated it casually, probably to make her feel better, but he shouldn't have done that. "Does he think I'm stupid or something?" She'd remembered muttering to herself when he'd said it. But she knew that's not what he thought." Darn. I wish I would've been nicer to him that night. And you know what, Janice, all is not well with the world!" She loved admonishing herself.

And that's when the phone rang. "Hello."

"Hi Janice. It's me. Mikey."

"Oh my God, Mikey. How are you? Are you ok?" There she goes.

"I'm fine. Sorry, I probably shouldn't called but I was . . . " she interrupted.

"No, don't say that. I'm glad you called. I was worried about you."

"One more week and I'm out of there. Janice, I had to do this. I had no choice. I love these guys. I know that's probably hard to understand but these are my homies."

Janice had begun to tear up, but she didn't want him to know that. Fortunately, he kept talking. That's all she needed to regain her composure.

"Mikey, when you get back, I want to invite you for dinner at my place. I used to be a pretty good cook, you know. Do you like kraft dinner?" She waited. No response. "Just joking. I'll make hot dogs instead. Or maybe Kraft dinner and hot dogs. How about that?" She started giggling.

"I'm quite sure that anything you make will be superb. It's a date." Oops, did he just say that? "I meant . . . "

"She decided to save the drowning man. "I know what you meant. Let me know when you're available so I can make plans. For the date, I mean." She couldn't help herself, and she began giggling. He joined in. Both knew they'd have pleasant dreams this night.

ONE MORE WEEK

IKEY'S DREAMS WERE indeed pleasant, and when he awoke the next morning, he was on cloud nine. He'd been so afraid to call Janice. He must've picked up that phone ten times before he finally let it ring through. And now they were going on a date, Kraft dinner and all!

Still giddy from the dreams of the night before, he did something he normally didn't do. He let down his guard. It couldn't have been more than a minute. But that's all they needed. Crap!

The first blow caught him just below the ribs. He reacted instinctively and brought his arms up to protect his head. And then what felt like a bat slammed against his back, driving him to his knees. He covered up as best he could, knowing this was going to get a whole lot worse. But it didn't. Not for him. He glanced up just in time to see Enrico and two of his boys lay out his attacker.

"You ok?" Enrico to Mikey.

"Yeah. I'm fine. I'm sorry man. I screwed up." Mikey.

Enrico helped Mikey up. "Still gotta go? We're coming with you." And they did.

Mikey had broken the rules. Had the boys not arrived when they did, he would probably be another statistic right now. "So much for that date!" He shook his head at his own stupidity.

Oddly, the guards were nowhere to be found. Obviously, they hadn't cleaned house completely. But that's ok. Their time was coming. "Find out who it was." Mikey to Enrico. "No problem." And it wouldn't be.

His foolishness could have wiped out everything they'd been working for these past months. "Damn that was stupid!" And it wouldn't be the last time he'd chastise himself. "I really want to go on that date!"

They found the rat. Upper management dealt with that issue, and they made sure the prison population knew it. Mikey knew he had to make an appearance. It gave the other inmates strength and hope. If he can take it, so can we. But we gotta stick together.

The final days of Mikey's stay were uneventful. But they'd all learned a powerful lesson, and the inmates were beginning to trust management, at least a little. It'd always been them against us. It still was but something had changed.

And finally it was over. They hated to see him go but everyone of them would've walked through those same doors to freedom given the chance. Mikey had gone way above and beyond the call of duty for them. Now it was their turn. Besides, Mikey would be back from time to time anyway. They'd do him proud. And they did.

DATE NIGHT

"WHY CAN'T I QUIT sweating?" Mikey was having problems. He never sweat this much even when the crap was being beat out of him last week. But this was different. He was going on a date. He'd never even been on a date his entire life! "Relax. Just relax." To himself. "Calm down. It's just Kraft dinner and hot dogs, for Gods sake." But that didn't help one bit. So he changed his shirt for the third time, glanced in the mirror for the twentieth time, and headed out the door. One quick stop. No. Better make that two. What had O'Malley said? Oh yeah. "You can't go wrong if you pick up a bouquet of flowers and a bottle of wine. Don't be cheap now. You hear." He heard, and he followed O'Malley's advice to a tee.

He took a deep breath. Checked himself out in the mirror one last time, and with wine and bouquet in hand, headed up the sidewalk. He pushed the buzzer and waited. Nothing. One more time. When the door swung open, he gasped. He couldn't help himself. "My God, she's gorgeous!" To himself. He started to say something. And then he tried again. Thankfully she read the situation perfectly and put him out of his misery.

"You shouldn't have! They're beautiful. And this will go perfectly with dinner. Come in."

"Thank you." That's as far as Mikey got.

"Dinner isn't quite ready yet. Let's have a glass of wine while we wait. Red or white?"

"White please." Mikey, smarten up. Relax for Gods sake!

Fortunately, Janice was a talker. Within a few minutes, Mikey was all in. "God, I feel good around her." Of course, to himself.

It turned out that Kraft dinner and hotdogs weren't on the menu. "Darn. I was looking so forward to it." Mikey was on a roll now. "Thanks for inviting me. I wasn't sure if you'd ever talk to me again."

He shouldn't have gone there. The mood quickly changed but Mikey was able to save the day. Or should I say, date. "I brought alone a CD I thought you might like. Do you mind?"

As the music filled the room, Janice's mood began to change. Her favourite artist. How did he know that? He's so sweet.

He'd escaped that time. Mikey, watch your mouth.

They had a great evening. And finally, at midnight, they said their good nights. Mikey wasn't quite sure how to handle this part but fortunately, Janice rescued him once again. She embraced him slightly, gave him a peck on the cheek which he reciprocated, and bade him good night. And as he walked down the driveway, some would say skipped down the driveway, she yelled after him. "That was fun. We need to do it again sometime. Night, Mikey."

"Yes!" And he skipped down the driveway. She watched from the window. And giggled. Like a school girl.

O'Malley couldn't wait to hear how Mikey's date with Janice had went. "Geez, its midnight. Where are you?" He had to laugh at himself. When had he ever got home at midnight when he was dating? Thirty minutes later his patience was rewarded. "Here he comes. Pretend you're watching TV." Crazy old man.

"When he heard Mikey whistling as he walked up the driveway, he knew this'd be good. "Calm down boy. Calm down."

"Hey O'Malley, you're still up. Whatcha watching?"

He would ask that, wouldn't he? "Nothing really, just flicking the channels, killing time."

Mikey knew what O'Malley was up to. Maybe he'd just play along for a bit. "I'm headed for bed. See you tomorrow."

"Wait. Would you like a coffee or something?"

"No, I'm fine." Ok, I'd better give him a break. "On second thought, I will have a cup of coffee. Thanks."

O'Malley was quick to comply, and once they were both settled in, Mikey decided to give the old man a break.

" I had the best time of my life. I picked up flowers and wine, just like you said. She loved them."

"And?"

Mikey had to laugh. And we ate a wonderful home cooked meal."

"And?"

"And we listened to music most of the evening. And we talked. That's all."

"That's it?"

"Oh I'm sorry. Was there something else I was supposed to do? You must not have marked that down. I checked off everything you said. Wine, flowers, music. What'd I miss?" And then Mikey began to laugh. "I'm sorry. I'm teasing. O'Malley, I had the best time ever. Happy?"

He was. Very. "That's my boy!" Under his breath. "I'm going to bed now. Night."

O'MALLEY IS KIDNAPPED

I F MIKEY THOUGHT the problems at the prison were over, he was severely wrong. He'd pissed off a lot of people and if he thought they'd take that lying down, well, get ready. Plans were made. Two of their best outside men were recruited. The date was set. Mikey thought he had them beat? Never!

O'Malley had a full day of sailing under his belt. "What a great day." To himself. As he was preparing his Tom Cat for its nightly sleep, he noticed a van edging itself towards him. He thought nothing of it. Vans go by here all the time. But when it stopped right in front of him, it got his attention. One look at the two characters approaching him and he knew this was not going to end well.

He was right. The gun in his ribs convinced him that he best comply with their demands. "Punks! If I was younger I'd wipe the floor with you!" But he wasn't so anything he was thinking he kept to himself.

"You're coming with us pops."

"Pops! Who the hell you calling pops?"

That's when he went to sleep. A pistol across the side of the head can do that to you. When he awoke, all he knew for sure was that he was in a heap of trouble. They had bound him to a chair and now that he'd woke up, they were ready to get to work.

But first they had a call to make. "Mikey, listen up. We have O'Malley. If you ever want to see him again, you'll do exactly as we say. Got it?"

Mikey nodded into the phone. "What do you want?" Like he didn't know.

"Here's are demands." And they read them out. "You have two hours." And with that, the phone went dead.

Mikey sunk into the chair. "Not O'Malley. What am I going to do?" And then he knew and he made the call.

"Derek, its Mikey. I need your help." He explained it as quickly as he could. "Please help me. They'll kill him. I know these guys."

"Ok Mikey. Don't do anything until I get there. Don't tell anyone else. No one. Are you hearing me?"

So Mikey waited. "Hurry up, Derek. For Gods sake!" The minutes seemed as hours. And finally Derek pulled into the driveway.

"Did they call back?"

"No. But I wrote down their demands. They'll call back, right?" Mikey was beside himself.

"They'll be calling. Mikey, you've got to keep them on the phone as long as possible. They might give something away. You've got to be calm." Derek was ever so calm. He shouldn't be the one here. This was an active case; he was cold case but it wasn't time to squabble over jurisdictions. Save that for later.

And then the phone rang. "Done yet?"

"I want to talk to O'Malley before I do anything. Put him on the phone now!" They hung up. "Oh my God. What'd I do?"

"Relax. They'll call back. They need you, remember?"

And it did ring again. Derek cautioned Mikey again. "Stay calm. Relax."

Mikey answered it but before he could say anything, the caller informed him that perhaps he should check out the photo he'd sent. And then he hung up again.

They flipped to the attached photo. Derek knew what to expect. Mikey recoiled at the sight. It was O'Malley alright, the parts of him one could see through all the blood. "These guys mean business." Derek.

"I'll kill those bas . . . I will!" Mikey was even scaring himself.

"Mikey. They'll be calling back right away. You need to calm down. I need to look at that photo again. I'm going to grab my laptop from the car. Here's my email. Forward the photo to me. I need to see it on a bigger screen. Mikey, now!"

Mikey complied. He was trying his best, but if they killed O'Malley, he'd get them. One way or the other, he'd get them!"

And then the third call came. "You taking us seriously yet, Mikey? Now you have an hour. Don't screw this or he dies!" And he hung up once again.

"They called back. He dies in one hour, Derek. If we give in to their demands, we lose the prison. But I can't lose O'Malley! I can't."

"Mikey. Look at this." Derek had uploaded the photo to his computer.

"Why would I want to look at it again? I don't want to see him like that."

"Mikey. Look. Tell me what you see. Not O'Malley. Forget about him for a second."

Mikey was getting it. "Ok. I see some red neon lights I think. Up on the right corner. See?"

Derek did see it. "Can you make out the letters? Tell me what you see?"

"I think it's an A and maybe an S. There's another letter above it but it's only partially showing. I'm not sure what it is."

Derek was starting to get excited. "Mikey. Look closely. Could it be a G?"

"I guess it could be. Yeah maybe. I bet it is. GAS, That's what it is! Derek, what're you thinking? Derek?"

"I know that place! I know where it is! We gotta go now!"

Derek wasted no time. He called for backup and he and Mikey made their way down to the warehouse district. Derek had worked these streets for years. There wasn't a building he didn't know. They were all the same, these punks. He must've visited this area a thousand times over his career. "Gotcha!" Under his breath.

Mikey just stared at Derek. How the hell could he know the location from two letters on a sign, in a city of millions of people? How was that possible? "God, I hope you're right!"

They approached the building from the backside. He killed the engine and the lights and opened the trunk of his car. "How much time until they call back?"

"About thirty minutes."

"Ok, we can't wait. Here." He handed Mikey a bat.

"You're giving me a bat? Give me a gun, for Gods sake!"

"Right. Like I'm going to give you a gun. You'd probably shoot me. Take the bat or stay here. It's up to you." And with that, Derek began making his way down the back alley. Mikey followed, bat in hand. "And don't talk. Not one word?"

"Yes sir. Anything you say, sir!" Under his breath. Sitting in the car had absolutely no appeal. None whatsoever.

That's when Mikey noticed the sign. He motioned to Derek but Derek was way ahead of him by this time. He knew its location and he knew how to get into the building undetected. He motioned for Mikey to be absolutely still. "Not a sound. If they don't know we're here, O'Malley has a chance. If they hear us, they just might shoot him first before they get the hell out of there. Come on."

They made their way inside. And that's when Mikey saw O'Malley. He looked bad. Mikey fought to restrain himself. Derek motioned for him to relax, breathe. Mikey nodded. Derek made his move.

And that's when one of the punks saw Derek. He swung his gun around but it was too late. And the next second he was lying dead on the floor. The second man bolted for the door and that's when Mikey stepped up to the plate. The bat broke when it made contact, but not before it shattered the knee cap of the would be killer. And that's when the backup arrived. And that's when Mikey ran over to O'Malley.

He was hurt bad. But he was a cop. And he was tough. "Untie me for Gods sake!"

O'Malley would be fine. But for now, he was headed for the hospital. Under protest, mind you. Too bad! They kept him for two days before kicking him to the curb.

All he was really worried about was his Tom Cat. He hadn't even got it put away before they attacked him. Hope it's still there! Of course it was. Mikey had made sure of that as soon as O'Malley was tucked safely away in the hospital. O'Malley should have known that.

And more heads would find their way to the chopping block inside and outside the prison walls.

DEREK RETHINKS HIS CAREER

EREK TRIED TO THINK back to when he'd last felt the rush he'd gotten taking down O'Malley's captors. That certainly didn't happen in his time with the cold case squad. He loved the results they were getting but he had to admit, there wasn't much of an adrenalin rush. But when he was called in to do the paperwork on an "active" file which he was the lead on, he knew what he had to do.

Fortunately, this was a department that took care of its own. Leave the fighting to the other guys. We all have a job to do. Let's get it done! So when Derek stepped out of bounds on the warehouse case, it wasn't that big of a deal.

So he wasn't sure why they'd called him in again. Presumably to talk about the case. Whatever. He showed up at the appointed time. He was whisked into the the office of the Chief of Police. "Derek, have a seat." He wasn't alone. The Assistant Chief, as well as the Deputy Chief were also present. "Odd." Thought Derek.

"Derek, we've been following you for years."

"Me? Why?"

"Not just you. We know what a bang up job you're doing in the cold case division. It's great. But we also know the job you did when you were with homicide. And you've been pretty active lately in a couple of pretty high profile cases. Derek, we want you to consider coming back to homicide. We need more guys like you. It's totally up to you, but we'd sure like you to think about it."

That was it. Derek left the building practically walking on air. He'd been thinking the exact same thing. He'd enjoyed the past five years or so but that last case involving Mikey, well that showed him how much he was missing. He still had a lot to offer, and now they were approaching him! I'm going for it! But then he remembered that he had to talk to Claire first. They'd just come through, and were still going through, some very tough times. But one of the things they had absolutely agreed on was that they needed to communicate better. This would be one of those times.

"Claire, we need to talk."

She was immediately scared. "What's up Derek? Is there something wrong?"

"No, God no. The opposite. Remember, we said that we'd make important decisions together? Well, I have an important decision to make, and I want your input."

"Ok." Wow, Derek was taking this stuff seriously. So was she. The difference was that it was usually her that all those discussions were about. "This is good. I like it." To herself as usual.

"Let's meet for dinner tonight at the usual place, if that's all right with you? About eight? I've got a bunch of running around to do until then. Will that work for you?"

"Yeah, that's fine. See you then. Love you!"

"I love you, too. Bye." And with that, he was gone.

CLAIRE DOES A 360

"THIS SHOULD BE INTERESTING." Claire mused while waiting for Derek. He had something he wanted to tell her, and she had something she wanted to pass by him. This communication thing was working after all. In the meantime, she may as well sit back and relax. Derek sounded excited on the phone so it must be something good. And what she had to tell him she was quite sure he'd readily embrace. She sipped on her wine while she awaited his arrival.

They'd come close to blowing up their marriage. Truth is, she'd come close to throwing it all away. Derek had been an absolute prince the whole time. How he'd put up with her this long, she didn't know. Thank God she'd gone to see Pastor Rick when she had. And her boss. He'd kicked her butt so hard that she could still feel it. The truth hurt. It hurt like hell but she needed to hear it.

She thought the pastor would be a little more sympathetic towards her, but nope. He didn't kick as hard as her boss but he didn't exactly pull his punches either. "You want your marriage? Then fight for it. Derek's doing his part. In fact, he's carried the both of you for over four years now. Step up sister." Wow. Lots of sympathy there! But, he was right, of course. She'd stepped up. And she'd be stepping up a whole lot more after tonight.

"Hi hon. Sorry I'm late." Derek apologized.

"That's ok. I was just sitting here thinking about how much I love you. I really do, you know."

He knew. And she knew how much he loved her. They would survive.

They ordered and then, unusual for Claire, she asked him to tell her his news first.

"Really? Ok. Hon, I was called into the Chief of Police's office today."

"Oh my God! Is everything ok?"

"Let me continue."

"Sorry."

The Deputy Chief, and the Associate Chief were there as well." Claire stirred but never said a word. Derek was choosing his words carefully. "Claire, they asked me to rejoin Homicide. They said they loved my work and that they'd been watching me over the years. They have a position for me the moment I'm ready."

Claire studied Derek carefully. She could tell he was excited. Derek didn't get excited about very much. He was like a kid sitting on a tack. She knew he needed her support. Crap, she didn't like that idea one bit but how could she tell him that? So instead. "Hon. What do you want to do? What's your gut telling you?" Like she didn't know.

"Hon. I've loved solving cold cases, but when Mikey and I caught O'Malley's captors a few weeks ago, I hadn't felt like that for a very long time. I loved it! And I'm good at it, Claire." He's such a puppy dog. Her man, the full grown puppy.

"Derek. You have to follow your heart. Good God, I've certainly followed mine! But I can't lie, hon. It scares me. The thought of you lying dead in the street terrifies me. I don't know if I could handle it. I'm sorry. I'll support you 100% in whatever you decide. I will. I promise. But I had to tell you that."

"I know you did. And trust me, I understand. Just think how I felt when I didn't hear from you for days on end, and you don't even pack a gun! Remember, I've trained my whole life for this, and I've worked homicide for years. I know what I'm doing out there. I need this, hon. I really do."

She knew that. This was her husband. And she'd stand by his side. No matter what.

Tomorrow he'd be heading down to headquarters. With his wife's tacit approval.

Claire didn't know what Derek wanted to tell her, but she wasn't expecting that. He was like a kid in a candy store. She wanted to tell him he was crazy. That it wasn't fair to his wife. But she couldn't. She saw a light in his eyes that she hadn't seen before. He had to do what he had to do. Like she did.

And now it was her turn. "Derek, I have something to tell you as well."

Under his breath. "Please be something good. Please."

She knew what he was thinking. Women know these things. "Hon, it's all good. Seriously. I've been doing a lot of thinking as well. It's time I gave something back to my industry."

She paused. He listened. "Go on."

"I've been talking to my boss about becoming a mentor to a couple of reporters in our office. It's time. I need to step back a bit and let others take the lead. It's been all about me for far too long. And I nearly lost my husband in the process. I can't lose you Derek." Tears began welling up but she continued. " Derek, you know I love the work I do, and I probably always will, but it's time. My boss is on board. To be honest with you, I don't think he quite believes me. I'd have to fly back and forth to Houston for a couple of days per week for the first few months, and then it'd only be once a week after that. What do you think about that?"

Derek was stunned. She'd do all that to save their marriage and she'd mentor some other reporters! "Claire, I'm so,proud of you. Oh my God, that's great!" He meant it. But isn't it ironic? She steps away from the abyss while he rushes towards it. What a crazy world!

SUMMARIZE EVERYTHING

I T ALL STARTED WITH JASON, a terribly conflicted young man that could see no way out of his present situation. Except one. And that decision led him to the depths of hell, and hopefully, back. That would be between him and God. But despite everything, he had managed to find his one true love, Janice.

She was an absolute delight. Everyone loved her. A single mother that turned a precarious situation into a career as a writer featuring her own beautiful daughter, Joline. She taught Joline well, and she would grow up to be a strong, independent woman, taking on the world's causes as if they were hers. She had become a seasoned world traveller, and a well known blogger, but she still found plenty of time to spend with her Mom.

And then through circumstance, Claire, a fiercely combative investigative journalist, came to Seattle, on a course, but really to spend time with Derek, who at this time, was a member of the Cold Case squad. They'd met a year prior but neither had made a move. Until now.

And that's when Claire looked into her own files long since buried. In a time well passed, when she at 11 years of age and her brother, Mikey, had killed their father. Their mom died soon after, and Claire was sent to a foster family; her brother, to prison.

And then a case caught her attention, and suddenly the adoptive family she had walked a way from shortly after college, were thrust back into her life. She knew she had hurt them deeply when she walked away, but now she was back, and she would make amends as best she could.

Jason's screw up had placed Janice in an untenable situation, and her family might well be killed. Fortunately for Janice, Derek caught the cold case, and he shared it with Claire. And that's why she had no choice but to come clean, and God willing, save her adoptive family from certain death.

Pandora's box had been opened the moment she looked into her own file, and all was not as she had been told. That's when she met her brother, supposedly a thing of evil, but decidedly not. Claire was a fighter and soon Mikey would walk out of that place a free man.

But Mikey was a man of principle, and had become a pastor on the inside under the tutelage of Charlie, lifer turned pastor. He would mentor Mikey, protect him, and love him, as if a father.

Mikey was now a free man, but his heart was on the inside. He would not abandon those who had sought his counsel on the inside. So he became part of the pastoral prison system and worked unceasingly to reform a system that was rotten. That would result in multiple death threats that only furthered his resolve.

There were others who came along side all of the above characters to shape them into the people they have become today.

JOLINE AND ERIN'S BIG ADVENTURE

EVER SINCE JOLINE HAD watched The Way, starring Martin Sheen, she knew that one day she'd make that same trek. She remembered being fascinated at the thought of a pilgrimage, done alone, and yet with thousands of participants in search of themselves. In days past, and still today for some, the pilgrimage was/is done simply to reach the tomb of the Apostle Saint James the Great. This was not for the faint of heart, and yet not that difficult if one was in reasonable condition. But it was long, nearly 500 miles in total before Santiago de Compostela would bade them stay and rest awhile. Well done.

There are many tour operators in this area that make the trek much more agreeable for the majority of travellers, but the more hardy among us like to do it on their own, or with a few companions. Accommodations are sparse along the route, blisters are common, the psychological makeup of the seekers of self, diverse, to say the least. But, what an accomplishment for those so inclined.

Joline was so inclined, and she'd went on about it forever to Erin, and finally convinced her to come with her on this journey of a lifetime. "Just think." Joline would rave. "A pilgrimage. How can't you be excited?"

Erin was not convinced that she needed to walk 500 miles in order to find herself, but Joline was so convincing that she decided to go along. Either they'd be even better friends at the end, or they'd never want to speak to each other again.

And that's what they did. The trek began at St. Jean Pied de Port, in France and would conclude the official portion in Santiago de Compostela, Spain. They were in great condition since they were avid hikers anyway, but it would still take them a full month to complete the pilgrimage. That's where they would receive their "Compostela certificates" which signified that one had done the Camino de Santiago. They had duly registered at the Pilgrim's Office when they began their trek, got the appropriate stamps along the way, and now stood in line to receive their compostela and a protective cylinder. They had been asked the reason for their pilgrimage, and both had declared it was for religious or spiritual purposes. The next day they would participate in the Pilgrim's Mass, and fortunately, they were there when the Botafumerio was brought out. It's incense filled the air while the Hymn of Santiago was sung. A religious experience may not have been their prime reason for making the trek but that's exactly what they got.

But of course that wasn't good enough for Joline. If Martin Sheen could make it all the way to Finisterre, so could they. Three days later they dipped their toes into the Atlantic Ocean. Even Erin had to concede that Joline was right.

They stayed there for three more nights and then made their way back to Paris, where they'd stay for a couple more days before heading back to Seattle.

They did the usual tourist thing in Paris, but what intrigued them the most was the sidewalk cafes, particularly those with a view of the Eiffel Tower. With that as a backdrop, people watching became their sport. They had walked quite enough by this time, thank you very much.

So they sat, and sipped coffee most of the day and well into the evening. And people watched. They marvelled at how well they dressed here. And they looked each other up and down and shook their heads. "We're a couple of slobs!" And they laughed until they cried.

"Stop it. I'm going to pee my pants." And with that first and foremost in her mind, Joline headed for the bathroom. "Watch my purse." And then she heard what sounded like an explosion, and people screaming. Suddenly smoke filled the room. She headed for the door. But she already knew what it was. That thing that you force to the back of your mind. What are the chances? "Please, God, not Erin. Please God." She made her way through the smoke to the street. Past bodies and body parts strewn about. And to where Erin was supposed to be. But she wasn't there. "Erin! Erin! Please God!" At the top of her lungs. And then she saw something moving from under the canopy. "Please God. Please God." She kept saying it over and over. Others had joined her looking for survivors. They found three of them under the collapsed canopy. It was too late for one of them. The other two were quickly pulled from the rubble and into the waiting ambulance. Erin was one of them. "Please God, don't let her die. Please."

Joline wanted to call her Mom. But she couldn't. Her phone, along with everything else she had on her that day, was obliterated in the blast. Five people would lose their lives that evening, and scores more would suffer debilitating injuries. Some were more fortunate. Like Joline. Taking a bathroom break at the exact right time. Erin wasn't as lucky. But still luckier than most. The canopy had collapsed on top of her and the other two just before the second blast went off. That's all that saved her.

Erin wasn't exactly feeling very saved. Her ribs were crushed by the falling canopy, she had a concussion, and massive bruising over her entire body. But, she hadn't lost any limbs, and she was alive.

The news reports would confirm that there were two blasts, probably set off by the same individual. He was most likely among the dead, but that was yet to be confirmed. Five were confirmed dead, one American among them. There were, at last count, at least a dozen with severe injuries, and dozens more with minor cuts, scrapes, and so on. Updates to follow as we learn more about this terrible tragedy.

That's what Janice heard when the song on the radio was abruptly cut off and replaced with a news bulletin: Terrorist attack in Paris! Several dead; one American among them; scores of injuries! We will continue to update as more information becomes available! And that's when she tried to phone Joline. Nothing. "Oh my God. Joline. Answer! Answer your phone!" Nothing. "Do I have Erin's number? Yes."

She tried it. Again, nothing. "Please call me baby. Please." She couldn't stop the tears.

Joline had called her early this morning to let her know their plans for their last day in Paris. "Mom, we're just going to hang out for the day. Drinking coffee and eating bagels and watching all the fashionistas strut their stuff. Mom, the sidewalk cafes here are awesome."

She knew Joline would call if she could, and that's what was driving her nuts. "I need to hear from you now!" She tried to relax. There was nothing she could do but wait. And that's the hardest thing in the world to do. She tried to recall their earlier conversation. They had both purposely not talked about the possibility of exactly what had just happened. Like not talking about it would make it less real. But then she remembered their conversation. Joline was so excited. "Mom. I have something to tell you."

"Tell me."

"Nope. I need to tell you in person. Sorry." Teaser.

"At least give me a clue."

"Nope. You have to wait. I want to tell you in person." What a brat!

Janice's imagination went into overtime after that discussion. If it was that important, why didn't she tell me over the phone? She said it was personal. Ok, what's that mean?

Staring at the phone wasn't working, so on impulse, she forwarded the home phone to her cell, and headed to her parents. She didn't want to alarm them but she couldn't be alone any longer.

They'd already heard the news but hadn't phoned, knowing full well that Janice would've been waiting for Joline's call. "Have you heard anything yet?" She shook her head in the negative.

And within minutes Derek and Claire pulled in behind her, grim expressions on their faces. One more vehicle was making its way down their street. Mikey knew where to come as well. This was, and would always be ground zero as long as these two were alive.

So they waited in silence. There was really nothing to say. The television spit out the same news time and time again. No updates. No names released.

And then Janice's phone rang. She stared at it, not recognizing the number. Finally. "Hello."

"Mom, it's me. I'm ok, but Erin's hurt real bad." Joline was obviously crying on the other end.

To everyone in the room. "It's Joline. She ok, but Erin's in bad shape. Baby, do you have a number we can call you on? This one?"

"No, not yet. My phone was destroyed in the blast, along with our bags. We'll begin working with the Embassy tomorrow to arrange passports, travel arrangements, and so on. I just borrowed this phone to call you. As soon as I get to the hotel, I'll call you with their number. Hopefully I can get another phone tomorrow. Mom, Erin could've died." Janice could hear Joline crying.

"I know, baby. But she's going to be ok. Right?"

"Yes. Mom I've got to go be with Erin. Tell everyone that I love them. Love you Mom. Bye."

Janice put the phone down. Everyone was waiting. "She's not doing well." Janice could not stop the tears running down her face. "She's really worried about Erin. I wish there was something I could do."

Claire put her arms around Janice. Granny and Gramps bowed their heads in prayer, and soon the rest did as well.

What else was there to say? There job now was to wait. Wait for Joline's next call.

MIKEY COMFORTS JANICE

B Y NOW THE FAMILY had accepted Mikey as one of their own. Which made his relationship with Janice somewhat awkward. He wasn't sure if he should hug her or shake her hand. Fortunately she made that decision for him. "Mikey, thanks for coming." And she gave him a hug. There. That wasn't so hard, was it?

But now Janice wanted to go home. She'd keep everyone up to date. "Mikey, would you like to come over for awhile?"

"You bet." She always made things easy for him. "Damn, I like this woman!" To himself.

So they left, and Derek and Claire soon followed suit. "Quick hugs all around. At least Joline was safe. And her friend.

"Mikey, do you mind if we just drive around for a bit? I hate it when I have to just wait! It's the worst! Let's do something. Anything. Please."

"Let's just drive around. It might be hours before we hear anything." So that's what they did. For hours. Seven to be exact. But, if that's what it took. Certainly better than pacing the floor all day.

Finally Janice conceded that enough was enough. It was nearly 8 pm here, so that meant it was nearly 5 am in Paris. They wouldn't be hearing anything more for at least a couple of hours. "Mikey, let's go home."

Janice was glad Mikey had shown up at her parents. She wanted them to get to know him like she did. He had a way of calming her down without even saying a word. He seemed to know that there was no need for small talk. Just being here with her was enough for him,and truthfully, for her as well.

Now was certainly not the time, but they both knew that one day they were going to have to have a serious discussion. About them.

"Mikey, do you mind if I go to bed? I'm exhausted."

"Of course not. I'll check on you later."

"Mikey, I know I shouldn't ask you this, but I'd really appreciate it if you'd stay the night." And that's when she noticed the strange look on his face. She burst out laughing. "I meant in the spare room." And she burst out laughing again.

His red face had said everything she needed to know. "Of course I will. I knew that." No he didn't. Not a chance. "Do you mind if I watch some TV?"

"Anything you want. Fix yourself a sandwich if you'd like. Help yourself to anything you need." And off she went.

That was embarrassing. He sunk into the sofa. And that's where he'd stay for the rest of the night, if necessary. He'd grabbed a pillow and blanket from the spare room, stripped down to his tee shirt and briefs and made his home in front of the tv. Sleep did not come easy, but no matter. She wanted him here. And that was good enough for him.

But the TV finally lulled him into a deep slumber. He awoke with a start. Janice was gently shaking him. "Do you mind?" And she slipped in beside him. "Hold me." Hesitating, he cautiously embraced her. She snuggled in closer and within moments she was fast asleep. He wasn't, and he wouldn't be for the rest of the night.

As the midnight hour approached, Janice began to stir. She shifted her body so they were face to face. She snuggled even closer, head on his chest. She reached up and stroked his face ever so gently. He dared not move. She lifted her head up slightly and kissed him ever so gently. Then she settled in once again. That's how they would stay for another hour. And then the phone rang.

Janice jumped up and reached for the phone. "Hello."

"Hi Mom. Just checking in."

"Hi baby. How's Erin?"

"She's not doing very well at the moment. She'll be in the hospital for a few more days yet. Mom, I'm staying here until we can come home together. She needs me. I just wanted you to know."

"Of course, hon. I'd do the same. Do you need anything? Should I fly over? I could be there by tomorrow."

"No Mom. I'm fine, and besides, I'm at the hospital all the time anyway. I just wanted you to know. I gotta go, Mom. Love you. Bye."

And then she was gone. Janice understood. She would've done the same thing. She looked at Mikey and began to giggle. He looked at her. "What?"

She looked him up and down, and that's when he realized that when he'd stood up, the blanket had fallen to the floor. She had to admit, he looked pretty hot in that tee and rather tight briefs! Having a red face in this woman's presence was becoming a given! He shook his head, grabbed the blanket and headed for the spare room.

"Mikey." She yelled. I'm going back to bed. In my bed. See you in the morning!"

He decided that maybe he'd just stay in the spare room after all. He doubted he'd be getting much sleep this night anyway! But he must have, because she tapped on his door to let him know that breakfast was nearly ready.

"Ok, give me a few minutes."

Now fully clothed, he returned to the living room and a still giggling Janice. "Breakfast is served, your Majesty."

She was obviously in a great mood. Apparently she had got enough sleep. He wasn't sure anymore whether he had or he hadn't, but he'd play along anyway. Why thank you, my Queen."

They settled in, nary a word was spoken, and ate their breakfast. But it was the coffee that brought him back to life. And reality. He remembered he had an appointment in less than two hours and he still needed to go home and shower, shave, shampoo, and all the rest, before then.

"I'm sorry but I've got to get going. I'll call you later, ok?" And with that he made his way to the door.

She followed him, and as he was about to exit, she threw her arms around his neck, drew him closer to her, and kissed him, and not the gentle kiss of the night before. "Call me later, ok?"

Absolutely!

THESE THREE THINGS

EREK AND CLAIRE WERE in the best space that they'd been in since their marriage. It'd taken a few body slams to get Claire fully on board, but thankfully, she finally got it. In fact, she had no idea just how close she'd come to losing him. He wasn't about to tell her either.

And then, when she decided to become a mentor to not one, but two promising reporters, Derek knew she was serious. And the reporters? They couldn't believe their good fortune. Her boss was elated. Shocked, but over the moon.

They'd been close for years. He'd never had a better student; she had never had a better teacher. But she'd lost her way. She wasn't just good, she was great, but she'd begun to take unnecessary risks. The story was never worth more than one's life. He told her that time and time again. She always agreed, but they were just words, and the next big story would always take her into situations that time would have eventually solved. But she was impatient. She wanted it now. And she got it. But with each success, she grew bolder. He feared for her life constantly, and then she stepped over the line once too often. A man died as a result. He probably would have anyway. But she could have died as well that night. In fact, she should have. But it changed her. Thank you, God, was all he could say. Thank you, God!

Derek was another story. He'd made the choice to go back to the homicide squad. He was a great detective that had reached burn out status but decided to work cold cases instead of quitting entirely. He was a fabulous asset there as well, but as time went by, he knew he was missing the excitement that only homicide could supply. Recent events, and especially the attention of the upper brass, forced him to reconsider his options. And now that Claire had stepped back from the edge, he knew what he had to do. Claire certainly had her misgivings but she wasn't about to try and talk him out of it. Besides, one look into his eyes and she knew he was exactly where he wanted to be.

So that would be the framework upon which they built their lives. They had great careers, a beautiful home, vehicles they enjoyed, and enough income to live comfortably. "Derek, we've been pretty blessed, haven't we? But I was thinking, what else would I want, or you, to complete our lives? You know, like maybe more vacations, or a cottage by the lake, or some fine art work . . . I don't know. Whatever. What would you want?"

Derek had to think about that. He wasn't a huge "stuff" person. He generally bought what he needed. Of course, a really well equipped library would be nice, or perhaps a wine cellar, or . . . ?

Claire was having fun with this, and she could tell that he was thinking about it. "I'm grabbing some paper. Give me a sec." she returned to the sofa where they'd retreated to flick channels, with two pens and paper in hand. "Here. One for you and one for me. Ok, here's the deal. Write down three things you'd most want, and I'll do the same. Then you try and guess mine, and I'll try and guess yours."

Derek rolled his eyes but decided to play along. "Ok, but I bet you'll never guess mine." And with that they got to work. This was proving to be more difficult than they thought. Suddenly, this wasn't just a game anymore, they were getting downright serious.

"I'm done. You?" Derek was done first. A moment later, Claire was as well.

"I know. You write down what you think I'd want on the back of your list and I'll do the same." They got busy. This was kinda fun.

They laid that list face up so both could see their spouses guesses. And they were both wrong. "Boy, we don't know each other very well, do we?" Claire was slightly taken aback. "This is getting interesting." Derek agreed.

"Ok then, Derek, tell me one of yours and then I'll tell you one of mine."

"Ok, I'd love to have a Boxer."

"What's a boxer?"

"A dog, silly. I would love to have a dog."

"Hmm. Ok, that's easy enough, I guess. Ok. My turn. I'd love to have an art studio in my home. Just a small one."

"Really? I never knew you liked art. Go figure. It's not like we don't have the space. Interesting." Derek was getting to know her.

"Next."

Derek piped up. "I want you to go first this time."

Oh boy. "Derek, I know we haven't talked about this. But it's really been on my mind lately." He could tell she was reluctant. "In fact, the next two items are kinda the same, actually."

He glanced down at his list. He was pretty sure he knew where this was going. "Mine too. Claire, turn your list over. I'll do the same." They stared at each other's lists for the longest time, neither saying a word. And then he reached out to her, and her to him, and they held each other tightly. Tears streamed down both their faces. They did know each other after all. And there was certainly enough room for a Boxer and an art studio too.

In that incredible moment, there lives took on another dimension. Logistics? We'll figure it out together!

MIKEY'S APPOINTMENT

WHAT MIKEY HAD failed to mention to Janice was what his appointment was about. It was his life after all, not hers. He felt guilty the moment that thought crossed his mind because, like it or not, he needed her support. He needed her a whole lot more than he wanted to admit. If he was really being honest with himself, he'd have to admit that he was falling in love with her. Falling? Too late, he already was!

"That kiss! I know she likes me." He was scared to take that thought any further. And besides, it was time to go. This meeting could determine which way Mikey's life went over the next several years. "Crap, I should have talked to her about this." But now it was too late.

Mikey's social experiment at the prison had attracted a lot of attention. Drug traffic was down to a crawl, inmate deaths and injuries were a fraction of what they'd previously been, and the inmates were doing most of the policing themselves. Costs were minimal. Morale had gone through the roof. In prison? How was that possible? No one wanted to believe it was a God thing, but the facts were speaking rather loudly. First it was Charley. It was still a pretty crazy place back then but he had his followers, and when Mikey came along, and eventually took over from Charley, real change was in the air. They'd tried their best to shut him down but he wasn't afraid of them. Mikey had a huge following. He understood them and they understood him.

But then the impossible happened. Mikey became a free man. That should have been the end of it. The Big Dogs thought they'd be back in charge the moment those jail doors slammed shut with Mikey on the other side. God, were they wrong! This was Mikey's home. He wasn't about to give up control so easily. And that's when he asked to go back inside to mentor some of his followers. If they stood united, they could beat these punks at their own game. Upper management was all in as long as Mikey understood the risk. It would be on him; not them!

He understood the risk. And he nearly died for it. But he didn't. And now his two interns were in charge under his direction, and they too had a substantial following. Plus Mikey would continue to make weekly visits. The removal of a few guards and a management change had completed the picture. Several months had since passed with only minor issues arising. As far as upper management was concerned, it was a success. Now they wanted to duplicate it in other prisons around the country and they wanted Mikey to lead the charge.

So when he left the meeting only moments ago, only one decision remained. "Will you do it? Will you lead the charge? It'll mean going inside from time to time to establish a core group of followers. It's incredibly dangerous. There's no way to sugarcoat it. We'd understand if you say no. Think about it for a few days. We'll meet back here next Friday at the same time." And then the meeting was adjourned.

He'd been the one proposing the above. Now it was put up or shut up time. He wanted to deny his excitement but he couldn't. This is what he was put here for. This is why he'd spent thirty long years in prison. For this very moment. This is where God wanted him.

But he knew he'd never be able to explain this to Janice. Perhaps he didn't need to tell her everything. Right. If she asked, he'd tell. My God, she'd practically went postal on him when he went back inside for those two weeks! And, he hadn't even told her about the attack.

The ringing phone startled him. He glanced at the number. Janice! Crap! "Hello." Calm as a cucumber.

"Hi. Just wondering if you'd like to go out with me tonight?" And then she added. "On a date."

"On a date? Yeah, you bet. Should I meet you somewhere, or . . ."

"I think you should pick me up."

"Ok. Great. Should I make a reservation somewhere?"

"I already have. See you at 7 then?"

"See you at seven. Bye." Mikey shook his head. "What have I done?"

DEREK AND CLAIRE MAKE AN APPOINTMENT

FOR THE NEXT SEVERAL days that's all they could talk about. And the more they talked the more convinced they became that they could indeed be great parents. It was obvious that they would adopt, and equally as obvious to both of them that they wouldn't be adopting babies. Not a chance!

The more they talked, the more obvious it became that they were on the same page on this issue. They both wanted the opportunity to help shape a young life, or lives if they were fortunate enough to adopt siblings. There preference would indeed be siblings, preferably a girl and a boy, but that would remain open ended.

Claire knew something about adoption obviously, since she was adopted herself, and she knew what she'd put her parents through, especially after she'd graduated from high school. She couldn't bare the thought that their child/children could do the same to them. Even now, after all these years, she still couldn't understand why she had walked away from a family that truly loved her as one of their own. But one thing seemed to over ride everything else: that sense that some how she didn't belong.

Derek had lost his parents at an early age, but by then he was already out on his own. He had learned how to handle loneliness well, but always envied his friends that still had their parents in their lives. He often marvelled at how much they took their parents for granted.

He, on the other hand, would have given anything to go home just one more time. But he couldn't. The car crash ensured that.

But he was as excited as Claire was. She'd told him her story on numerous occasions, and her fears, but she'd also shared with him her dreams and aspirations for these yet unknown children. But, she made it abundantly clear, it would be their kids dreams, not hers or Derek's, that would take centre stage. Their role would be to support them, encourage them, course correct them from time to time, but especially to listen to them. And number one: love them, and teach them about God. Claire's words. Interesting!

So they made the appointment. They'd done as much research as they possibly could on line, and now it was time. The administrator was impressed with the amount of research they had done, plus of course, their credentials. And the fact that nationality would not play into their decision. But they did want siblings, preferably a boy and a girl and preferably 9/10 or older. That could prove interesting. But nothing was cast in stone. And they were ready now. From here on in, it would be in the hands of the Agency and God himself. "But if you don't mind, we'd like to check in once in awhile, if that's ok?"

Derek and Claire left the Agency practically floating on air. They were going to be parents! When exactly, they weren't sure, but that was no longer in their hands. All they had to do was be ready. And that, they were!

MIKEY AND JANICE'S FIRST "REAL" DATE

M IKEY WAS NERVOUS. This was the real deal. He'd peppered O'Malley with question after endless question. And now it was time. Finally, with one final glance in the hallway mirror, he headed for the door. O'Malley just shook his head. "That's my boy!"

He arrived at Janice's place at the appropriate time, rang the doorbell, and waited for her to appear. He tried his best not to stare, but damn, she was ravishing. "Sorry, but I'm a man!" To himself. She sensed his nervousness and quickly took his arm. He immediately relaxed, remembered O'Malley's instructions, and escorted her to the car where he opened the door for her, ensured he wasn't going to smash her leg in the door, and closed it at the appropriate time. "Whew!"

She directed him to the quaint little restaurant that she had picked specifically for this occasion. She knew he was falling for her, and she couldn't deny that she was heading that direction nearly as quickly as him. She wanted this to be special. Quiet, unobtrusive, just the two of them. An intimate venue.

It was a wonderful evening. The food was sumptuous, the wine was divine, the dessert, decadent. And the company? Second to none!

The hours passed as if minutes, and begrudgingly they stepped out of their fantasy and into, in Mikey's words, "your chariot, my dear." Perfect.

He walked Janice to her door, unsure of his next move, but she knew hers. "Would you like to come in? For a drink."

"I probably should go." Mikey wasn't sure how to handle this.

"I'd like you to stay." She added. "If you'd like to."

To himself. "Like to? My God, I dreamed of this!" But to her. "I'd love to, but I can't. I hope you understand." And to himself once again. "She'll never talk to me again!"

But that wouldn't be the case. She understood immediately his dilemma. "What was she thinking? He was a Pastor, for God's sake!, Janice!" She admonished herself.

"I'm sorry Mikey. I wasn't thinking. I understand. Really, I do. And then she added. "And I respect you for it. Nite, Mikey." And if he thought the kiss the other morning was special, well, it paled in comparison to this one! "Call me tomorrow, ok?" And with that she went inside.

Mikey stared at the closed door for the longest time. "Yep. I'm in love." Finally, he made his way down to the waiting vehicle, opened the door with a flourish, and that's when everything changed.

They were waiting for him. They had their assignment. And he was it. Hurt him bad. But don't kill him. Not this time. Make sure he understands that we know where his girlfriend lives.

He sensed something but it was too late. A steel pipe across the side of the head can do that to you. He remembered going down to his knees and he remembered getting booted in the face. And that's when he passed out. They must have continued beating him, because when Janice found him he was covered in blood.

Janice had already jumped in bed when she remembered that she'd left the outside light on. She glanced out on impulse. Mikey's car was still in the driveway, the driver's door wide open. "Oh my God, Mikey!" She grabbed the phone, opened the door cautiously, and then hurried to where Mikey was laying half in, half out of the car. "Mikey." He barely responded. She dialled 911. "Hurry! He's in bad shape." She gave the operator the particulars, hung up and immediately called Derek.

The ambulance and police arrived moments before Derek and Claire. "Mikey was sitting up by then, but resisting the attendants efforts to help him. Janice was doing her best to calm him, but to no avail. Derek stepped in, and the moment Mikey saw him, he relaxed. "Ok, fine. But I'm not staying." One step at a time.

The police agreed to meet Mikey at the hospital but first they'd question Janice. That took all of thirty seconds. Derek and Claire waited for her to get dressed. You can come to the hospital with us. Besides, Derek wanted to ask her a few questions without anyone else around.

Derek knew Mikey wouldn't tell the cops a whole lot, so he'd let them do their thing first. Then he and Mikey would have their own little chat, once they were alone. Janice knew nothing. They'd said good night, she'd went in to get ready for bed, he'd headed home as far as she knew. Thank God she'd forgotten to turn off the outdoor light when Mikey left. She shuddered at the thought of it. It wouldn't be the first time she'd left that light on all night. "What if I hadn't checked?" Over and over to herself. Derek didn't tell Janice that he'd arranged to have a patrol car park across the street for the night.

Mikey was a mess. He never saw it coming. "My head hurts like hell!" They questioned him over and over. "You must have seen something. Do you have any idea why they attacked you? Did they take anything?"

"I don't know. Check my clothes. My wallet should be in my jacket pocket." They checked. It was. Nothing appeared to be missing. "Are you sure you don't know who attacked you? Does your girlfriend have a jealous ex, maybe? Something doesn't fit."

"Are you suggesting that I staged this or something? That I'd smack myself over the head with a pipe? Give me a break." Mikey was obviously perturbed. Let me rest. If he knew anything, he wasn't giving it up. "Ok, fine. We'll drop by tomorrow."

Finally it was Janice's turn. But not to question him. She just wanted to hold him. That didn't turn out to well. He was hurting real bad. "I'm ok, hon. Why don't you go home? I'll be better company tomorrow."

She knew he was right. "Ok, baby. Love you." What had she just said?

Mikey couldn't help himself. He broke into a huge grin that lit up the room. Derek and Claire exchanged glances. Claire gave Janice a big hug, bade her brother good night, and ushered Janice towards the door. She'd take Janice home and Derek would stop by later. He'd get a patrol car to drop him off. But first, he and Mikey would have a little chat now that everyone was finally gone.

"Ok Mikey, talk." These two understood each other.

"I never saw it coming. The next you know I was on the ground. One of them was stomping on me and the other one kept smashing me with the pipe. I covered my head as best I could but it didn't do much good. Derek, they told me they had a message for me. And I'd better listen up real closely. "Kill the plan now! You know exactly what we mean! And, we know where your girlfriend lives. The next time we come, it won't be for you! Understand?"

Derek, You have to help me. They'll kill her. I know these guys!" Mikey grabbed Derek's arm. "Ouch! Geez, man!"

Derek caught that last statement. "You know these guys?"

I know who their bosses are. And, Derek, I saw the tattoo on the mouthpiece's neck. I'd recognize it anywhere. Derek, I want that piece of garbage. You need to help me!"

"I will. You didn't tell the cops any of this?" Mikey should his head in the negative. "I figured as much. That's why I stuck around. We'll get them but we have to be smart about this. Ok? You gotta tell me everything you know. Everything. Deal?"

"Yeah. Deal."

"Ok, I'm out of here. I'll see you tomorrow. Oh, I've got a patrol car parked across from Janice's place for the night."

"Derek, don't tell Janice, ok. Not yet. I'll tell you everything to-morrow."

So he headed back over to Janice's place. After ensuring that Janice would be ok for the night, he and Claire headed home. Claire wasn't fooled one bit. "Tell me what's going on."

There was no use pretending around her so he brought her up to speed as best he could. Including what Mikey had "forgotten" to tell the cops. "Derek, I'm scared. Mikey's in way over his head. And now Janice's involved whether she knows it or not."

"I know babe. Mikey told me he'd tell me everything tomorrow." And with a flick of the switch, the garage door welcomed them home.

THE DEALS OFF

MIKEY AWOKE WITH A START. "Oh God." Everything hurt. He glanced around the room. "What's going on? What're you doing here?" The three board members looked downright glum.

"Mikey. We got an anonymous call telling us that we'd find you here. The caller also said that next time we'd find you in the morgue." And then he hung up. Mikey, we're killing The Plan."

"Because of this? Then they win. I'll be fine." Mikey was peed.

"Mikey, listen. There's more." He took a deep breath. "They got Enrico."

"What do you mean. They got Enrico. Who got Enrico?" But he knew.

"Last night. Around midnight. He's dead, Mikey. They left a note on his body. Kill The Plan or this was just the beginning. And they knew about you, too. You were both set up. "It's over man. Sorry."

Mikey couldn't stop the tears from rolling down his face. Enrico was like a son to him. And now he was dead. And it's my fault. "Please leave. Please." Not another word was spoken as they exited the room. Derek saw them go, and he saw Mikey trying to wipe away the tears.

"What's wrong? Mikey, tell me." And Mikey did. Every last detail. As he talked, the tears flowed.

AND THEN CAME THE CALL

"CLAIRE, ARE YOU SITTING DOWN?"

"What's wrong? Who's this?"

"Claire, calm down, this is Agnes, you know, from the Agency. I have some news for you."

"Sorry Agnes, I'm just always on edge, Derek's work and all. Sorry again." And then Claire realized what Agnes had just said. "What news?"

"We have a possible match."

"A match for us? Agnes, for us?"

"Yes. I need you and Derek to come down to the office this afternoon if you can. We need to go through the profiles together, but I'm positive that these kids could be a perfect fit for you."

"Oh my God, did you say kids? More than one?" Claire was practically climbing the wall.

"Yes, a brother and sister. He's 12, she's almost 11. They've been in the system for over a year now but the foster parents contract is coming up next month. We think you would be perfect for these kids. I've met them, Claire. You're gonna love them!"

Claire was already crying. "I already do, and I haven't even met them yet! I have to call Derek." We'll be there this afternoon! Guaranteed."

She could hardly dial the phone, but she finally calmed down enough so that when Derek answered, she could play it cool. "Hi hon. Whatcha doing?"

Weird. "I'm working. It's a work day. Why are you acting so strange?" He shook his head.

And that's when she screamed into the phone. He practically jumped out of his skin. And when she told him the news, he screamed as loud as she had, freaking the hell out of her. He quickly glanced around. Thank God everyone else had left for lunch. He hadn't told a single soul that they were going to adopt. Not until it was done, at least. "Yes. I'll meet you there at 2!"

"Thank you God. Thank you." And he could not contain the tears that flowed down his cheek. "Finally, we can be a real family."

WE'RE COMING HOME

FINALLY! "MOM, WE'RE COMING home. We'll be arriving on Saturday. I've missed you so much!" Joline could no longer control her tears. She'd sucked it up long enough. She had to. She had to be strong for Erin.

Janice was in the same space as Joline. "Thank you, God." Was all she could say. Over and over, and "I'm picking you up. I won't take no for an answer!"

"I'll get Erin's room ready for her. Is there anything . . . "

"Mom. No, mom. We have a place. We're rented an apartment for a few months until Erin recovers. It was easier that way and besides, we didn't want to bother you." Joline knew her Mom wasn't going to like this one bit. And she was right.

"Why would you do that? I have plenty of room. You know that." Janice was getting more perturbed by the moment.

"Mom. Erin's injuries were worse than we thought. I'm up all hours of the day and night with her. We thought this was the best solution. Don't be offended. Gosh. I'm trying to do what's best for Erin. I thought you'd understand."

Janice understood alright. God, she wanted to ask Joline some questions that had been bugging her for awhile, but now was not the time. Instead. "I'm not offended, hon. I just thought that you'd be coming to my place. That's all. You caught me by surprise. Sorry."

"Mommy, please don't say that. I know you're going to be helping us bundles anyway. This just seemed to make the most sense, that's all. And Mom, can you come alone to the airport? We'll get together with everyone once we get settled, ok?"

And that's how they left it. As usual, more questions than answers. "God, I can't wait until we can have a face to face conversation!" And under her breath. "I wonder if it has one or two bedrooms?"

DEREK AND CLAIRE'S BIG VISIT

EREK AND MIKEY HAD become close friends, much to Claire's delight. But she wasn't sure if they were sharing everything with her. Not that it was really her business, but once a reporter, always a reporter.

They seemed to have their secrets, and that frustrated her to no end. Fine! Be like that! But for now, her mind was on the kids. "Oh my God! Our kids! Ours!" But what she had failed to tell Derek was that this was not yet a done deal.

The current foster parents could decide to permanently adopt the children themselves. They had stepped in the previous year shortly after the tragedy that took the children's parents, and had fostered them ever since. Agnes had cautioned Claire to keep her expectations to a minimum until they knew for sure. Claire had refused to hear that part, and she didn't think it was worth mentioning it to Derek.

She should have. Derek met her at The Agency precisely at two. He practically ran up the steps. Claire and Agnes were waiting for him, but neither seemed as excited as he obviously was. "What's up?"

"Come in." Agnes took them into her office, poured them a coffee, shuffled a few papers, and that's when Derek piped up. " We're not getting the kids, are we?"

Claire looked away but not before Derek saw tears streaming down her face. "What the hell's going on? You told me they were ours." He was livid, but trying to stay in control.

That's when Agnes took over. "Derek, the current foster parents just filed an application to permanently adopt the children. We didn't see that coming at all. But that's their right, and since the kids have been with them ever since the tragedy, they've become a real family. They have four kids of their own, so we expected it to be temporary, but as far as they're concerned, they're already their kids. And apparently, the kids are already calling them Mom and Dad."

She paused. Derek sat in stunned silence. Claire kept saying "I'm sorry, baby." over and over.

Derek finally spoke. "Claire, you told me it was a done deal. Why'd you do that?" At that moment he was a defeated man.

"I was so excited. I should have told you. I'm so sorry. Please forgive me." She reached for his arm. He shrugged her off.

"I have to go back to work." And he left her sitting there with Agnes.

"I have to go too." And she scurried after Derek. "Derek, please! Let's talk. Please."

He knew it wasn't her fault. He knew he shouldn't have acted like that back there. She came to him. He wrapped his arms around her. And they cried. Agnes watched these two from her office, and she too, could not contain the tears. "Please don't give up. There are so many other kids that need you. Please." All to herself.

MIKEY'S NEXT MOVE

ONCE MIKEY GOT OUT of the hospital, he immediately met with the Board. They were adamant that The Plan was dead. No one would endorse it now; hell, they'd had to fight tooth and claw to get it to this point, and now with their lead guy sitting in the hospital because of a beating, and his lead man inside now dead it was over. Forget it! In fact, it's more than over. You can't go back to the prison anymore. Period.

Mikey walked out of there a broken man. He'd worked so hard. The guys inside had worked so hard. For what? For nothing, that's what? And now he'd abandoned them. He hadn't, but how'd they know that!

Someone was going to pay. "As sure as God is my witness, I'll get them! Me, a Pastor, what a joke!"

So he called Derek. He told him everything. Mikey wanted information that he knew Derek could ferret out. "I want their names, Derek, and where they live."

Mikey was pushing Derek into a corner. "What would you do, even if you knew? You can't take the law into your own hands, unless you plan on living on the inside again. Is that what you want? Let us do our job. Are you hearing me?"

Mikey was hearing exactly what he wanted to hear, nothing more. Derek couldn't help himself. "Like Claire." He muttered to himself. "Go figure."

And this is when Derek and Mikey would split the sheets. Derek had already included Mikey on one occasion that he shouldn't have. But, time had been of the essence then, and O'Malley was still with us. But that was different. Now Mikey was hell bent on revenge. Sorry, buddy, ain't gonna happen.

"Mikey, you're a good man. Don't screw that up. I'll take care of it. I promise." But even as he said it, Derek knew that Mikey was already tuned out. He didn't like where this was going and there wasn't a damn thing he could do about it! Well, one thing. Catch the punks before Mikey found them!

JANICE CONFRONTS MIKEY

SHE'D GOTTEN TO KNOW Mikey pretty darn well over the last while. And she was hoping that this was just the beginning. But ever since that beating, and especially when he'd heard about his friend in prison being killed, he'd changed. At first she was shocked, but when he started going off on her, she reluctantly began to withdraw from him.

He didn't seem to care one way or the other. My God, what a change! A few weeks ago she'd have sworn that he was madly in love with her, and truth be told, she was falling fast herself. Now? He wasn't even the same guy!

And in some ways, he wasn't. Those pieces of crap had killed his friend, and they'd threatened to kill Janice. She didn't know that, and he wasn't about to tell her, but the threat was real. And they were going to pay! He'd get them if it was the last thing he ever did.

If that meant staying away from Janice, he'd do it. It was worth it. They'd gotten their way. They'd won. But that didn't mean they wouldn't be back. So Mikey began to withdraw from Janice. He blamed it on his deteriorating mental state. He was having a hard time dealing with Enrico's death, and the sudden closure of the prison ministry he'd worked so hard to establish. He told her all of that, and it was all true, but he didn't tell her the real reason he was acting like a jerk. And he wouldn't. She'd been through enough with the Jason fiasco. That had nearly destroyed her. He'd make sure she didn't go through that again. Now he knew who they were. And he didn't need Derek to do what needed to be done!

HELLO CLAIRE

CLAIRE HAD LEFT The Agency in a state of disbelief. She'd been so sure that they would finally have a family! And seeing Derek react as he had, totally unnerved her. Her man of steel was every bit as vulnerable as she. Except that he just went back to work. Like nothing had ever happened. She didn't. And in the back of her mind she kept hearing Agnes' words. "There are other children that desperately need a Mom and Dad. Please don't give up." But that's exactly what they'd done, at least for now.

And then the doorbell rang. "I wonder who that is?" To herself. But there was no one there. And then she noticed the package on the doorstep. She looked up and down the street. She shrugged her shoulders, picked up the package, and went back inside.

It was addressed to her. "Strange. No postage." Maybe Derek's just goofing around trying to cheer me up. "Yeah, that's it!" But it wasn't.

It was dead at least. But those beady eyes stared at her as if they were alive. She gasped, then screamed. And that's how Derek found her. How long she'd been screaming, he didn't know. But he heard her the moment he pulled into the driveway. He opened the door, gun drawn. She stood there screaming at the top of her lungs. He involuntarily shivered, caught himself, holstered his gun, and approached her cautiously.

"Claire. Hon. It's me. Derek." But she didn't hear him. Or couldn't. And that butcher knife she held in her outstretched hand was scaring him. "Claire."

And that's when she swung the knife, barely missing his out-stretched arm. He grabbed her wrist, forcing the knife from her hand, and wrapping his arms around her. That's when she collapsed into his arms. They sunk to the kitchen floor. And that's where they stayed until the ambulance arrived. And the police.

EPILOGUE

CLAIRE

THERE WERE NO FINGER prints. Even the attached note had been wiped clean. The message was clear. YOU'RE A RAT! And the note made it quite clear: And soon you'll be a dead one!

Claire had crossed a lot of people during her investigative career. And now it was payback time. And this was added: I lost everything! So will you!

And all she could think of was: thank God we don't have kids!

MIKEY

He loved Janice. But he'd walked away. Now he knew who they were and where they lived. But first he had something else to do. Pastor Rick refused to accept Mikey's resignation. But here's what he'd do. "I'll give you three months of unpaid leave. Then we need to talk!"

JANICE AND JOLINE

These two were tight. But it was time to have that mother, daughter talk. Joline saw it differently. It was time to have a woman to woman talk. "Remember Mom, I'm not a child anymore."

DD ANDER's BIO

D ANDER never did fit in very well in the Prairie town he grew up in. While his classmates were settling down to careers and raising families, he was dreaming of mountain peaks and tall ships. And though he would attempt to follow these dreams, he would always end up back home on the prairies.

For a good part of his life he stayed the course, but eventually, he took his leave. He travelled extensively, and his experiences would soon catch up with his passion for a different life.

It would take him to places he should not have trod, and into experiences he should not have had. Stories would be told, by him, that he would deem fiction, but those who knew him, knew not where the fiction ended and the truth began. And they dared not ask.

He began to blog regularly during this time. Hundreds of blogs would follow, and to those who knew him well, it became obvious that the greater story lie between the lines. The public story was there for all the world to see, the other, for certain eyes only.

Although he lives in another part of the world today, he is always close by in one form or another. Whether through his blogs, photos, novels (fiction and non fiction), or one on one conversations, he is never very far away.

www. ddander.com

www.ingramcontent.com/pod-product-compliance
Lightning Source LLC
Chambersburg PA
CBHW070024260626
47159CB00005B/1942